A NEW LOOK

Amber hurried into the changing room. She quickly slipped out of her sweatshirt, T-shirt, and jeans and pulled the dress up over her shoulders. She straightened it around her hips, then zipped up the back. It fit perfectly. The dress was so glamorous, and so grown-up. She'd never owned a black dress before. Her mom always chose dresses in pastel blues or pinks. Amber felt about ten years older in black.

"Oh, Isabel. I love it!" Amber cried. She stepped out of the dressing room and twirled around. "What do you think?" she asked. "Is it what you wanted?"

"What do *you* think?" Isabel asked.

"It's absolutely perfect!" Amber said. She spun around again, letting the silky fabric swirl around her hips.

"You know what, Amber? In that dress you *look* like a champion," Isabel said.

Amber grinned. She felt like one, too.

THE ONLY WAY
TO WIN

Melissa Lowell

Created by Parachute Press, Inc.

A SKYLARK BOOK
NEW YORK • TORONTO • LONDON • SYDNEY • AUCKLAND

With special thanks to Darlene Parent, director of
Sky Rink Skating School, New York City

RL 5.2, 009–012
THE ONLY WAY TO WIN
A Skylark Book / June 1997

ISBN 0-553-48507-5

Published simultaneously in the United States and Canada

PRINTED IN THE UNITED STATES OF AMERICA
OPM   0 9 8 7 6 5 4 3 2 1

1

"Way to go, Tori!" Nikki Simon jumped up and down, punching her fists in the air. "You're doing great!"

"Awesome job, Tori!" Martina Nemo cheered.

"Fantastic!" Natalia Cherkas added.

Oh no, Amber Armstrong thought. I'm not late enough. I wanted to get here *after* the senior-level test was over.

Amber paused by the bleachers at the ice rink, almost hiding behind them. Tori Carsen was still on the ice, performing her routine. She was about to complete the test to become a senior-level skater. As Amber watched, Tori went into a spin, and the skirt of her sparkly white skating dress whirled around her.

Tori finished the spin, and a burst of applause came from her friends in the stands. She shook back her thick blond hair and waved, then smiled as she skated to the edge of the ice.

Amber swallowed hard. Tori had passed the test. That meant she would move from junior-level competition to senior level. Which meant that Tori could compete as a senior at the upcoming Sectionals competition. And then at the Nationals, and then maybe even at the Olympics!

No wonder all their friends were cheering!

I should be out there, Amber thought. I should be passing the senior-level test.

Tori slipped skate guards over her blades. She hurried toward the bleachers, grinning from ear to ear. Their friends ran down to meet her. Tori looked happier than Amber had ever seen her.

Haley Arthur noticed Amber waiting by the bleachers. Haley was a pairs skater. She had auburn hair and bright green eyes, and, at thirteen, was two years older than Amber. She was one of Amber's best skating friends.

"Amber, hi," Haley called. "Isn't it terrific? Tori passed her senior test."

"Yeah—it's great." Amber smiled faintly and curled a strand of light brown hair around her ear.

Haley gave her a sharp look, and Amber flushed. She wanted to be happy for Tori—she really did. She knew that Tori worked just as hard as she did and that Tori was a really talented skater. But Amber wanted to pass the senior-level test herself, wanted it so badly that it was all she could think of. But her coach, Kathy Bart, said Amber still wasn't ready. She said Amber needed a lot more practice.

It should have been *me* out there, Amber thought, watching Tori hug Martina, Nikki, Natalia, and Haley.

All six girls were members of an exclusive skating club called Silver Blades. The club was known for producing some of the top men and women skaters in the country. Amber was thrilled to be a member. She and her mother had moved all the way from New Mexico just to live in Seneca Hills, Pennsylvania, where the members of Silver Blades trained.

Amber was also thrilled to work with Kathy Bart, one of the best coaches in the country. Amber knew that working with Silver Blades would give her the help and the challenges she needed to become a top skater someday. But she couldn't wait for someday. She wanted to be at the top *now*.

"Come on, Amber. Let's get to it." Kathy's voice interrupted Amber's thoughts. Amber glanced up at her coach, who skated onto the ice and gestured for Amber to join her.

Kathy was the toughest, most demanding of all the coaches for Silver Blades. Her nickname was Sarge because she acted like an army sergeant. She barked orders at her skaters and never gave anyone a break. For Kathy there was no such thing as a "bad day."

But Amber loved working with Kathy. Amber took skating as seriously as Kathy did.

"Enough celebrating for Tori," Kathy said. "Time to get to work."

Amber wondered if Kathy could guess that *she* wasn't celebrating at all. She was too jealous.

Amber glided up to her coach. "Kathy? Can I ask you something?" she said.

"Sure," Kathy replied. She glanced at her watch. "But make it fast. We've already missed five minutes of practice time. And the auditions for the Greater Philadelphia Winter Welcome are coming up in a few weeks, you know."

The Winter Welcome was an important ice show in Pennsylvania. It featured the best skaters from around the state. Only two members of Silver Blades had been chosen to audition—Amber and Tori. And only one of them would get to participate.

"Well, that's kind of what I wanted to ask you about," Amber said. "I really need more time for private lessons. I need to polish my footwork, and then maybe I can take the senior-level test, too. Like Tori."

Kathy gave Amber a sympathetic look. "You're really close to being ready," she said. "And if it were just a question of time, we'd schedule more lessons. But you and I both know that it's also a question of money."

"I know," Amber muttered, staring down at the ice.

"I'm sorry, Amber," Kathy said. "But to get more time on the ice, we have to pay for it."

"You mean *I* have to pay for it," Amber said. The fact was that Amber's parents couldn't afford more private lessons.

A lot of the other skaters in Silver Blades had much more money than Amber's family. Her father had stayed in New Mexico. He had a good job managing a small factory there, but he would never be able to find the same kind of job in Pennsylvania. And he needed to earn money for Amber's skating. Both her parents did.

Mrs. Armstrong worked full-time at a real estate company in Seneca Hills. Sometimes she even took typing work on the side to earn extra money.

Amber knew skating was expensive. But she hated the fact that money was such a problem.

"Don't worry. You'll be ready for the test soon enough," Kathy told her.

"When?" Amber asked. "Tori can compete as a senior now. How will I ever catch up with her?" Amber pouted. "It's not fair! The only difference between Tori and me is money. Tori's family is well-off and mine isn't. She can get all the ice time she needs. She even has better skating dresses than me."

"What do dresses have to do with passing the test?" Kathy asked. "You're getting carried away, Amber. Besides, you know why Tori has more dresses than *anyone*. Her mom is a clothing designer, remember?"

"How could I forget?" Amber replied. Tori always wore extra-fancy skating dresses. She had dozens of them.

Amber had only one good skating dress that fit. It was turquoise and trimmed with yellow-and-white daisies. Her mom thought it was adorable. Amber thought it was totally babyish. She hated the thought of dragging it out for the Winter Welcome auditions. Appearance counted in auditions and competitions.

"I wish I could have a new dress for the auditions," Amber said. "Or at least have a new one by the time I take the senior test. If I ever take the test."

"Don't be silly, Amber," Kathy said. She shook her head impatiently, and her blond ponytail swung back and forth. "Of course you'll take the test. And soon, too. You just need to be a little more patient."

"I'm tired of being patient," Amber said. "Couldn't we get another grant from the USFSA?"

The United States Figure Skating Association had given Silver Blades a small amount of money. The coaches had divided the money among several Silver Blades skaters to get them extra ice time. Amber had been able to schedule three practice sessions because of it. But the money had run out pretty quickly.

"That money is gone for this year," Kathy told her.

"Then how else can I get more money?" Amber asked. "I mean, I can't get a part-time job. I'm too young. And I can't even baby-sit because skating keeps me too busy."

"I know," Kathy said. "Let's not worry about it, okay? Let's concentrate on your skating."

Amber sighed in frustration. "Okay. But sometimes this money thing makes me feel hopeless."

"It's *not* hopeless," Kathy said. "Since when do you give up so easily?" She suddenly grinned.

"Aren't you still 'gutsy Amber Armstrong'? The skater who was featured in *Sports Today* just last week?"

Amber smiled too, thinking of the magazine article. The writer had gone on and on about what a determined skater Amber was. She had called Amber one of the best up-and-coming skaters in the country. Amber was really proud of that article.

"They put a great picture of you in the magazine, too," Kathy reminded her.

Amber suddenly frowned. "Yeah—right under the picture of Tori," she said. "And I wish the writer hadn't made such a fuss about money. It was embarrassing. I don't want everyone in the world to know that my family is poor."

"Don't be embarrassed. Be proud that your family was willing to make sacrifices to get you into Silver Blades," Kathy told her.

"I *am* proud of them," Amber replied. "But how proud will they be if I don't pass the senior test? And I won't if I don't get more ice time, and—"

"All the more reason not to waste *this* time," Kathy interrupted. "Start your warm-up, Amber. I want to see you win that role in the Winter Welcome."

"Okay, okay. But don't forget that Tori is competing for that role, too," Amber pointed out. "And Tori might have a better chance because she's a *senior* skater now. And I—"

Kathy grasped Amber's shoulders and turned her toward the rink. "And *you* need to do your warm-up!'' she said in a stern voice. "And then meet me at center ice. We need to straighten out your triple salchow.''

Amber groaned. "Do we ever!''

"We'll get the salchow ready for the audition—don't worry. And don't worry about money, either,'' Kathy added in a gentler tone of voice. "I wasn't rich, and I had a successful skating career. So will you.''

Amber nodded. "Thanks, Kathy.''

"Now, hurry up. You've wasted enough time talking,'' Kathy said, glancing at her watch with concern.

Amber shook her head and skated off. She circled the rink with long, precise strokes to loosen her muscles. She was surprised that Kathy had let her go on even that long.

Amber knew that Kathy wanted her to win a big role in the ice show—almost as badly as Amber herself did. But how could Amber compete against Tori now that Tori was a senior skater?

"Come on, Amber! I want to see what you can do with that salchow,'' Kathy called out. "Time's a-wasting!''

No kidding, Amber thought as she skated to center ice. Time *is* a-wasting—and at this rate, I'll be stuck in juniors until I'm an old lady!

2

Amber dragged herself into the locker room and grabbed a towel. She wiped the sweat off the back of her neck. Kathy had worked her extra hard today. She had practiced jump after jump nonstop, and she was exhausted.

Tori was sitting on a bench in front of her locker, already changed into her regular clothes—forest-green leggings and an oversized sweater in the same green, with a deep blue pattern. The clothes were brand-new. Tori always had lots of new clothes, but these were new because Tori recently had experienced a growth spurt. She had shot up three inches and needed a whole new wardrobe of leggings.

Tori pulled on a pair of dark blue sneakers and glanced up at Amber.

Amber smiled at her, feeling a little nervous. "Uh, congratulations, Tori," she said. "It's great that you're a senior skater now. Sorry I didn't get a chance to tell you before."

"That's okay. Thanks," Tori replied.

"So . . . how does it feel?" Amber asked, sitting down beside her.

Tori shrugged. "It's no big deal, really."

Haley poked her head around the corner. "Don't believe her, Amber. Ten minutes ago she was dancing around the locker room like she'd just won a million dollars!" Haley jumped up and down, squealing and imitating Tori.

Tori laughed. "Okay, so I'm happy about it." She paused. "To be honest, I was a little worried that my new height would mess up all my jumps."

Growing taller sometimes threw off a skater's sense of balance, and she would have to work very hard to get her form back. Some skaters never recovered after a growth spurt and had to give up skating altogether. Amber couldn't imagine how awful that would be.

"Well, your jumps were perfect," Amber said. "So I guess you don't have to worry about it."

"I think it's great," Nikki put in. She was twisting her wavy brown hair into a thick braid. Nikki was fourteen and skated pairs with Alex Beekman. "You look more gorgeous than ever," she said to Tori.

"Thanks," Tori said. "I love being taller."

"And I'd love being a senior-level skater." Nikki

sighed. "Can you imagine how cool it will be when we're *all* senior level?"

"I'm tired of imagining," Amber retorted. "I've been doing *that* since I was eight."

"Don't complain, Amber. You're a fantastic skater. You'll definitely make senior. I don't know if I'll *ever* get there," Martina said. Martina was standing in front of the mirror, pulling back her jet-black hair with a clip. Martina was fifteen and skated singles. She really shone when she skated in front of an audience. But she wasn't nearly as good technically as Tori or Amber. She just couldn't get the jump combinations or spins that came so easily to them.

"What are you talking about? Of course you'll move into seniors," Haley told Martina. "I saw you land your triple toe–double toe combination today."

"Wow—you landed a triple toe?" Nikki asked in disbelief.

Martina grinned. "Hard to believe, isn't it?" she said.

Amber tried not to show her surprise. She didn't want to say anything, but she was as shocked as Nikki. Martina had been working on the triple toe for ages and had *never* landed it.

"How did you do it?" Tori asked. "I thought you still had major problems with that jump."

"I did," Martina admitted. "For months. Or is it years?" She laughed. "Anyway, if I tell you guys something, will you promise not to make fun of me?"

Haley arched an eyebrow. "That depends. How funny is it?"

Martina turned away from the mirror, her dark brown eyes shining with excitement. "There's this thing I just started to do for good luck. I try it every time I jump. And it works."

"Like what?" Tori demanded. She started to smile.

Martina shook a finger at her. "You promised not to laugh," she said.

"Sorry," Tori said. "It's just that I don't really believe luck has anything to do with skating."

"Come on, how can you say that?" Nikki asked. "You know that tons of skaters have little superstitious routines they go through before they skate. Even famous skaters. Brian Boitano always puts the same skate on first. And other skaters have lucky skates or laces, or—"

"Not just *famous* skaters," Haley interrupted. She opened her skate bag and pulled out a key chain. On one end was a bright purple fake rabbit's foot. "Some of us unfamous ones have good-luck charms, too."

Tori stared at Haley. "You mean you carry that thing around for good luck?" She shook her head. "I thought you were too cool for silly superstitions."

"Not me," Haley said with a grin. "I've had this ever since my first competition. Which I won," she added proudly. "I was six at the time."

"Then how come you never told me about it before?" Tori asked. Tori and Haley were best friends.

Haley flushed. "I guess I was kind of embarrassed," she admitted.

"You should be," Tori said.

Amber laughed. "Hey, I say if it works, use it."

"I agree," Martina said.

"So, what's your new good-luck charm?" Amber asked Martina. "A four-leaf clover?"

"No," Martina said. "Actually, all I do is wipe each skate blade with my thumb before I try my hardest jumps."

"You're kidding," Amber said. She leaned forward on the bench and rested her elbows on her knees. "That's all? And you landed a perfect triple toe for the first time because you did that?"

"Yeah." Martina shrugged. "I guess it relaxes me or something. I don't know. All I know is that when I forget to do it, I miss my jumps. They're horrible."

Tori made a face. "That's ridiculous. Your jumps work because you get them right. Not because of good luck."

"Not necessarily," Nikki said, twisting at something on her wrist. "See this? It's a lace from a pair of skates I wore the first time Alex and I did a perfect star lift. I've been wearing it ever since. I just tuck it under my costume so that no one can see it."

Amber gaped at Nikki. "I had no idea you guys all had good-luck charms." She almost felt left out. "That's really cool," she told Nikki.

"It's *not* cool," Tori declared, looking annoyed.

"It's silly. Can you imagine Michelle Kwan with some lucky skate lace or a rabbit's foot poking out of her sleeve?"

"Maybe she doesn't have a charm. Maybe she does some good-luck routine, like me," Martina said.

"What would you do, Amber?" Haley asked. "Carry a charm or do a routine for good luck?"

Amber shook her head slowly. "I don't know. I never thought about it before. I mean, sometimes I cross my fingers, but that's a little hard to do when you're spinning in the air."

Haley burst out laughing. "Can you imagine?" She started spinning around the locker room, keeping her hands behind her back with her fingers crossed. "Hey—I think I just invented a new move. I should name it after you."

"Yeah—the Armstrong *crash*," Amber said with a laugh. "But I wish I could come up with something that really works."

Amber thought about the auditions for the Winter Welcome. Good-luck charms might be silly, but she could use some extra luck right now.

3

"Tiffany? Hi, it's Amber." Amber leaned back on her bed and cradled the white phone under her chin.

"Amber *Armstrong*? The most promising skater in the entire world?" Tiffany Williams replied.

"Hey, no fair making fun of me," Amber said.

"I wasn't," Tiffany protested. "I just saw that article about you. My dad was reading his sports magazine and all of a sudden he asks, 'Tiffany, did you see this?' I couldn't believe it. It is *so* excellent. I mean, I know how great a skater you are, but—"

"But you were just stunned that you actually know me, right?" Amber teased. Tiffany was talking a mile a minute, as usual.

"Totally. I showed the article to all my friends, and they can't wait to meet you," Tiffany said.

"Yeah, I want to meet them, too," Amber said. She

and Tiffany were the same age. They lived in different towns, about thirty miles apart. They had met at an ice-skating camp called SummerSkate, where they had been roommates.

At first Amber hadn't wanted to be friends, because Tiffany wasn't as good a skater. Amber was more interested in hanging out with the older girls, like Tori and Haley. But then Tiffany had turned out to be a real friend. They'd been close ever since.

"So how come you don't sound excited about that article?" Tiffany asked.

"Oh, I am," Amber said. "I mean, I *was*, I guess. Until I went to practice today and Tori passed the senior-level test."

"Tori did? Before you? Oh," Tiffany said. "I'm sorry."

"I know I should be happy for her, and I am, sort of. But all I can think about is that I should be a senior-level skater, the same as her," Amber admitted.

"You will be," Tiffany said. "No problem."

"But it *is* a problem," Amber said. "Because I need more practice time and more lessons with Kathy to work on my jumps and stuff, or I'll never be ready for the test."

"Really? That stuff didn't stop you the last time," Tiffany teased.

"Ha ha, very funny," Amber said. At Summer-Skate, Amber had tried to take the senior test without anyone's finding out. At the last minute, though, she'd realized she wasn't quite ready.

"Tiffany, all the magazine articles in the world won't matter if I don't move up to senior competition soon," Amber said. "I can't let Tori beat me."

"Well . . . good luck comes in threes, right?" Tiffany asked. "So maybe the article is just the first thing. Maybe next your dad will strike it rich—and move to Seneca Hills!"

"I doubt it," Amber said. "Anyway, I think it's *bad* luck that comes in threes."

"Oh. I think you're right," Tiffany said. "Well, this should cheer you up. I'm planning a sleepover in a few weeks, and I want you to come."

"Really?" Amber asked.

"Sure. You can meet all my friends and forget about skating for the weekend. We'll have fun, fun, fun!" Tiffany said.

"Wow—a sleepover would be fantastic," Amber told her. "I haven't been to one since I left New Mexico. It sounds great! How many kids are coming?"

"About ten," Tiffany said. "Some are from my skating club, and some are friends from school. But you'll like all of them. And they've heard me talk so much about you, they can't wait to meet you in person."

"Wow!" Amber said again. "Thanks, Tiffany."

"For what?" Tiffany asked.

"For inviting me," Amber said.

"Like I wouldn't," Tiffany replied. "You're only the guest of *honor*."

"Do you want me to bring something to eat?" Amber asked. "Should I bring a sleeping bag? Oh no! We don't have a car."

Amber's father had kept the family car in New Mexico. Amber and her mom took the bus everywhere they needed to go in Seneca Hills.

"How will I get to your house?" Amber cried. "Oh! I know, I can take *two* buses to get there. Or maybe you can help me arrange a ride." She jumped to her feet, she was so excited.

"We can decide all that stuff later," Tiffany said. "It's not for three weeks, remember?"

Amber laughed. "Oh, right."

They chatted a few minutes longer, then hung up. Amber sprawled back on her bed and stared at the ceiling. Tiffany always made her feel so much better about things.

There was a knock on the bedroom door. "Amber? Are you off the phone?" Mrs. Armstrong asked.

"Yeah, Mom," Amber said. "Come in if you want."

Amber and her mom didn't have much space in their small apartment. They could only afford a place with three rooms. A small kitchen opened off the living room, and Amber had the tiny bedroom to herself. That way she could go to bed early while her mom stayed up typing or ironing. Mrs. Armstrong slept on the foldout couch in the living room.

Amber didn't really mind how small the apartment

was. She missed her dad. But it was also kind of fun to share the place with just her mom. And they worked hard at respecting each other's privacy.

"How's your homework going?" her mother asked, pushing the door open.

"Homework?" Amber repeated.

"You know. That school thing you have to do every night?" Mrs. Armstrong teased, ruffling Amber's hair.

"Oh, *that*," Amber said. "I did half before dinner. I'll hit the other half before it gets too late. But guess what, Mom? I just called Tiffany, and she invited me to a sleepover in a few weeks."

"That's great," Mrs. Armstrong said. "That gives you something really nice to look forward to. Only . . . how will we get you to her house?"

"Don't worry about that, Mom," Amber said. "We'll figure it out. We always do, right?" she asked.

Mrs. Armstrong smiled. "Right! We're a great team. Now, back to your desk," she ordered.

"Boy, you're starting to sound just like Kathy," Amber said. "But I can't call you Sarge—so I guess I'll have to call you Captain." She giggled.

"Actually, it's General. General Mom," her mother replied. She winked at Amber as she closed the bedroom door.

Amber threw herself into her combination spin. She was totally focused on staying in the same spot. She didn't want her skates to travel at all during the spin. The tighter and more controlled the spin, the more she would impress the judges. Not that there were any judges around today.

It was the following afternoon, and Amber was at group practice. Nikki and Martina were on the ice, working on their spins as well.

Amber came out of the spin and found herself staring directly at an older woman who was leaning against the boards. The woman wore a bright-red wool coat. Her lipstick matched it exactly. Her short blond hair curled against the collar of a white silk blouse. Three strands of pearls gleamed against her throat. The pearls matched her large, glittering earrings.

Amber blinked. The woman looked very stylish—and very rich. The woman tilted her head and smiled, looking right at Amber.

Amber had seen her enter the rink about half an hour earlier. The woman had gone directly to the boards at the south end of the rink, and whenever Amber skated by, the woman was smiling at her. It was almost as if she knew Amber. But Amber was sure she had never seen the woman before.

"Okay, guys. That's it for today," Kathy called.

Amber skidded to a stop, spraying ice shavings into the air. "Phew! If I have to spin one more second, I think I'll be sick," she complained.

"I know. Sometimes I get dizzy, too," Martina admitted.

Amber skated across the ice, stopped to slip on her skate guards, then headed toward the locker room with the others.

"Amber? Do you have a minute?" the woman in the red coat called out.

Amber stopped abruptly. "How do you know who I am?" she asked.

"I read an article about you," the woman said. "You're Amber Armstrong. I'm sorry—I should have introduced myself. I'm Isabel Hart. Call me Isabel." She held out her hand.

Amber stared at the giant ruby ring on Isabel's middle finger. "Uh, hi, Isabel," she said. She wasn't sure if she should shake Isabel's hand. By the time she decided to, Isabel had pulled her hand back.

"Listen, I know this seems weird," Isabel replied. "You don't know me, and I don't know you. But I was a skater once myself."

"Oh, really?" Amber said politely.

"Yes. And I know how expensive a skating career can be," Isabel went on. "The article mentioned that your family has made a lot of sacrifices for your skating. That's why I came here today. I want to offer you something."

"Like what?" Amber asked.

"Like money," Isabel answered, smiling. "I'd like to be your sponsor. That means I'd like to pay for your skating expenses, so you won't have to worry about money anymore. Are you interested?"

Amber gaped at her. "Interested?" she echoed. "Isabel, you wouldn't believe how interested I am! Tell me what I have to do."

4

"**Y**ou don't have to do anything but work hard and skate your best," Isabel told Amber.

"I already do that," Amber said.

Isabel laughed. "Of course you do. That's why I want to help you. I know how tough a skating career can be. But I also know you have the talent to succeed. It's important that nothing stand in your way—certainly not money."

"And you'll pay for everything I need?" Amber asked. She frowned. "What do I have to do in return?"

"Nothing." Isabel shrugged. "You do whatever's best for your skating. I buy you ice time, lessons, wardrobe—"

"New dresses? That would be awesome," Amber said. "I could use about *ten* new skating dresses."

"Then you'll have them," Isabel replied. "Maybe not all at once. But my job will be to get you the things you need."

"Wow. It sounds pretty good," Amber said. "Though I have no idea why you want to do it."

"Don't make me sound like I'm crazy," Isabel said. "Sponsors aren't that unusual, you know."

"I guess not." Amber had heard of other skaters whose expenses were paid by sponsors. Suddenly she giggled. "I never thought I'd have a sponsor all to myself."

"Well, I'd like to get involved in skating again, and this seems like the perfect way to do it. You need money, and I have money. Lots of it," Isabel told her.

As she stared at Isabel's jewelry, Amber almost asked how much. "You could probably do a lot for me," she said instead.

"I think so," Isabel said. "That is, if you want me to."

"If? I definitely want you to. This is like a dream come true!" She glanced over her shoulder. "But I guess I should ask Kathy—"

"I've already talked with Kathy," Isabel broke in. "She's very excited about my plan. Next we'll need to run this by your parents and get their okay. Kathy thought we could meet with your mother tonight to figure out the details. Does that sound all right?"

"My mom will faint," Amber stated. "She'll be so happy—you have no idea."

"We'll make sure she's sitting down first," Isabel

said with a smile. "But I'd like us to start right away. Your career's hot right now. We should build on that."

Amber's eyes glowed. My career? she thought. I like the way that sounds. In fact, Isabel sounded as determined as Amber always felt. This was going to work out perfectly—as long as her mother said it was okay. And why wouldn't she?

We'll never have to worry about money again, Amber thought. At least not for my skating. And with all the extra ice time and private lessons Isabel could pay for . . .

"This means I'll be able to take the senior test soon," Amber blurted out before she could stop herself.

"The senior test?" Isabel asked. "Is that something you're worried about?"

"Yes," Amber admitted. "I'm so close to nailing the moves I need. But I haven't been able to practice enough. You know how much ice time costs." She took a deep breath. "This is so weird. I was just talking about all this yesterday. And now, here you are!"

"You must have good karma," Isabel said with a smile.

"Karma?" Amber repeated. "What's that?"

"Oh, it's kind of a way to explain how things happen. For instance, if you've been working as hard as I think you have, then you've earned some good luck. Good things are bound to happen to you."

"If that's good karma, I want more of it," Amber said. "Having you show up to be my sponsor is just about the best thing that could ever happen to me."

Isabel shook her head. "The best things for you are all ahead."

"Like getting a part in the Winter Welcome show?" Amber asked. "I'm auditioning in a couple of weeks, and I really want to get the part. Only one girl from Silver Blades will get a role."

"Yes. I know all about the Greater Philadelphia Winter Welcome." Isabel nodded. "That would be good. But I was thinking of the more important competitions. I can see you taking the gold at Nationals, and later going to the Worlds."

"Wow! I think I can do that, too. I *know* I can," Amber said. "It's great that you have so much confidence in me." She paused. "Have you ever seen me skate in a competition?" she asked.

"No," Isabel admitted. "But if I didn't think you could win, I wouldn't be here. You have what it takes, Amber. And I want to be there when you get to the top."

"This is *so* awesome," Amber said. "So, what do we do now?"

"Well, why don't you go get changed? I'll set up a meeting with your mother and Kathy and we'll work out the details," Isabel said.

"Okay. I'll be right back," Amber said. She hurried into the locker room. She felt like jumping into the air. She had a sponsor!

Haley and Tori were inside the locker room, getting ready for their own lessons. Haley pulled a small hot-pink sweater over her head. Tori was tying her skate laces.

"Guess what, you guys!" Amber cried, rushing over to them.

Haley glanced up. "What's going on?"

"The most incredible thing just happened!" Amber exclaimed. "It's unbelievable. This woman—her name is Isabel, and she used to be a skater, and, well, she just showed up here today and told me that she wants to be my sponsor."

"Wow!" Haley exclaimed. "Your sponsor? As in—"

"As in, she's going to pay for *everything*," Amber said excitedly. "She thinks I can make it all the way. I mean, she's already talking about my competing as a senior skater at the Nationals, and then in the Worlds." Amber looked at Tori. "Isn't that great?"

"Yeah, sure," Tori said.

Amber put her hands on her hips. "You don't sound very excited for me."

"What am I supposed to say?" Tori asked.

"Well, 'Congratulations' would be nice," Amber said.

"Then congratulations. You're really lucky," Tori said.

"I *am* lucky!" Amber exclaimed. "Finally, I'm going to have all that stuff you've always had—private lessons, more ice time . . . I can't wait!" Amber gazed at Tori, who looked away.

"What's the matter?" Amber asked. "Hey, you're not scared about me being better than you now, are you?"

"Me? Scared of you? Get real," Tori scoffed. "Just because I'm not jumping up and down because you're getting extra lessons, it doesn't mean I'm scared of you."

Amber watched Tori thoughtfully. "Maybe not," she said. "But everyone at Silver Blades thinks you and I are the best singles skaters. And you're three years older than me. I just thought that must really bother you sometimes."

"Who said you're as good as me?" Tori started to raise her voice.

"Listen, Amber, tell me something," Haley said quickly, leaping between Amber and Tori. "How did this Isabel person hear about you, anyway?"

Tori turned away, and Amber shrugged. "Well, Isabel read that magazine article, the one about me and Tori and the other junior skaters," she explained. "Isabel used to be a skater herself. She knows how hard it is, you know, in terms of money and all that. She said she'll pay for all the ice time I want."

"That is fantastic," Haley said, grinning. "Amber, I'm really happy for you. You deserve it. Having a sponsor . . . I can't imagine how great that would be. Your life's really going to change, you know?"

Amber smiled. "I hope so." She flung open her locker and began pulling off her practice clothes. She couldn't wait to make all the arrangements for Isabel to start paying for things.

This is it, she thought. At last I'm going to have everything I ever needed for my skating. Now nothing can stop me from going straight to the top!

5

"**O**uch!" Amber yelped as she thudded to the ice. She had fallen on her triple salchow—again. She stood and brushed ice chips off her black practice leggings.

"I've just got to land this jump," she muttered. If only she could figure out what she was doing wrong!

Amber shook her head impatiently. Maybe she was just too tense. She bent over to stretch, touching the toes of her skates lightly with her index fingers. As she reached down, she almost lost her balance and felt herself move into a tiny spin. She stood up straight, then reached high over her head to stretch her arms.

"I'm *going* to land this salchow. It's now or never," she told herself firmly.

She stroked counterclockwise around the rink,

glided into an inside Mohawk, and launched herself into the salchow again.

One . . . two . . . To her surprise, Amber finished three full revolutions before she had even counted them. Her right skate touched the ice, and she glided smoothly backward, arms fully outstretched.

"I did it!" she shouted.

"Yahoo!" A loud cheer went up from the other end of the rink, followed by a shrieking whistle. "All right, Amber!"

Amber turned and spotted Haley and her partner, Patrick McGuire, who had been practicing their pairs spins. Haley waved her arms in the air. "You did it! You nailed the triple salchow!" Haley yelled.

Amber flushed. Martina, Natalia, and Tori were also on the ice, and now they stopped what they were doing to stare in Amber's direction. Amber was especially glad that Natalia had seen the move. Natalia had recently moved to America to join Silver Blades. She was from Russia and was a great skater. Natalia's salchows were flawless, and Amber tried to match Natalia's form when she practiced the jump.

"Six point zero!" Patrick called out, giving Amber an imaginary perfect score.

"Thanks, you guys," Amber called back to them, smiling. "I still can't believe I did it."

She glided to the side of the rink to rest a moment. She stopped near Martina and Tori.

"Did you ever land your triple salchow that well before?" Martina asked.

"Are you kidding? I've hardly landed it at all," Amber admitted with a laugh.

"I guess your extra lessons are already paying off," Tori said.

"I guess so," Amber replied. It had been a week since Amber's mom had agreed to let Isabel be Amber's sponsor. The first thing Amber had done was sign up for extra sessions with Kathy.

"How are those going, anyway?" Martina asked.

"Really well," Amber said. "I think Kathy likes having the extra teaching time. And Isabel is thrilled for me."

"Isabel and Kathy must make a good team, considering that jump we just saw," Martina commented.

"I guess," Amber said. "Mostly Kathy decides everything, of course."

"Of course," Martina agreed. "Can you imagine anyone telling the Sarge what to do?" she said, laughing.

"Well, Isabel is really encouraging, which is great," Amber said.

"Well, you'd better try that jump again," Tori said. "Just to make sure you *really* have it nailed."

"Oh, I think I do," Amber told her.

"I know—it was us, watching you, that helped you nail it," Haley joked, sticking her nose in the air. "Naturally, darling. That would make anyone do their best."

"Sure, having you guys around is the trick," Amber joked back. "After all, I couldn't land it until a second ago."

"Well, even extra lessons can't guarantee that you'll land it again," Tori told her.

Amber frowned. "I'll try it right now," she said. She circled the rink counterclockwise and again glided into an inside Mohawk. Before she could begin the jump, though, her skate blade caught an edge and she stumbled.

"Nice try," Natalia called, with an encouraging smile.

"Hold on—I'll do it perfectly this time," Amber called back. She frowned and began to stroke across the ice again, concentrating hard.

Now, what did I do wrong? she wondered as she prepared for the jump. I approached from an inside right edge and I . . .

She gasped. That's it! she thought. My own good-luck routine. *That's* what was different.

Amber skidded to a stop. "Wait a sec, you guys," she called to Tori, Martina, Natalia, Haley, and Patrick, who were all waiting for her to try the jump again.

Amber quickly bent down to touch the toes of her skates with her index fingers. She crouched and turned in a tiny spin. Then she stood and stretched her arms high over her head.

"Ready," she called again.

She built up speed, moved into the inside Mohawk, and took off—into a nearly perfect triple salchow.

"Way to go!" Haley yelled.

"That was even better than the other one," Martina agreed.

"Really nice," Patrick added as Amber skated over to them.

"So what did you do to nail it?" Haley asked. "Did Kathy show you something new?"

Amber shook her head. "It wasn't Kathy at all." Her eyes glittered as she faced them. "I found my lucky routine," she said.

Tori rolled her eyes. "Come on! You can't expect us to believe that. You didn't land a difficult jump because of some dumb ritual."

"Why not?" Haley demanded, hands on her hips.

"Yeah, I told you how a good-luck routine helped me," Martina argued.

"It's just a coincidence," Tori insisted.

"Okay, then how do you explain the way Amber landed her jump?" Haley asked.

"Please," Tori said. "It's because she's been working extra hard lately."

Amber felt a small surge of pride. That was almost a compliment, and Tori rarely gave out compliments.

"Good-luck routines and superstitions are only for skaters who don't believe in themselves," Tori added.

"Oh, really?" Haley teased. "Listen to her, Amber. She thinks we don't believe in ourselves. I think I'm insulted." Haley tossed her head, and Patrick laughed.

"Well, I'm insulted, too," Martina said, folding her arms in front of her chest.

"I don't care what anyone says," Amber said with a shrug. "All I know is that before I touched my toes, I was two-footing every landing. And after I touched them, it went fine. That has to mean something."

"Yeah—that you need to stretch more before you practice," Tori said with a snort.

"Ignore her," Haley said, resting a hand on Amber's shoulder. "She'll learn."

Amber grinned.

"Hey, we're going to the mall for a pizza. You want to come?" Haley asked.

"Me?" Amber nearly keeled over. The older girls hardly ever asked her to do anything with them outside the rink. It felt great to be one of the group for once.

"Sure! I'd love to!" she burst out. "I'll just call my mom—oh no!" she said.

"What's wrong?" Martina asked.

Amber groaned. "I can't go. My mom's coming by to get me in about five minutes. There's no way I can call to stop her."

"Oh. Too bad," Natalia said. "Maybe next time."

Amber nodded. "Definitely next time." She paused. "I guess until she comes, I'll practice that jump."

"Don't work too hard," Haley advised.

"Yeah, right," Martina teased. "You know Amber

will be here all night. Then she'll be here again to-morrow morning at six."

"No, I won't," Amber said. "I'll be here at *five*." She giggled, and everyone started laughing—everyone except Tori, Amber noticed.

Well, it wasn't her problem if Tori was jealous. Maybe now she'd find out what it was like to have some real competition.

"You're right, Amber. That triple salchow is much better," Kathy said the next morning.

"It looks fantastic," Isabel agreed. She was leaning on the boards, watching Amber's early practice. Isabel had begun coming to every practice. At first she had just watched, but now she was starting to give her opinion, too.

"I think your back left leg could be more extended on the landing," Isabel told Amber.

"Really?" Amber asked.

"Yes. Though I really see the improvement you've made," Isabel added.

"Thanks," Amber said, smiling brightly at Isabel.

"Right," Kathy said, clearing her throat. "Now we've *got* to work on your footwork, Amber. It's the last thing to fix before you take the senior test. Run through the sequence of rockers and Choctaws that comes halfway through your program."

Amber sighed. Why wouldn't Kathy give her credit for mastering the difficult jump, the way Isabel did?

Oh, well, Amber told herself. It isn't Kathy's job to give me compliments all the time.

She skated to the far end of the rink and began the footwork sequence, heading back toward Kathy.

"Wait—stop right there," Kathy cried, quickly skating over to Amber. "You don't have the flow right. You're still way too choppy."

Amber nodded. "I *thought* the rhythm felt off," she said.

"Start again. Go more slowly, until you can put it all together," Kathy instructed.

Amber skated back to the end of the rink, running through the sequence in her mind.

"Okay—let's see it," Kathy called.

Amber took a deep breath, then skated straight ahead, building speed as she repeated the sequence of tricky steps.

"Stop!" Kathy cried, holding up her hand.

Amber skidded to a stop.

"Just a minute, Kathy," Isabel called. "May I say something?"

"Certainly," Kathy said. She sounded polite, but Amber could tell she was a little irritated.

"Well, I know it's been a long time since I skated," Isabel began. "But it seems to me that it's confusing to do a footwork sequence *out* of sequence. Do you know what I mean?"

"No, actually, I don't," Kathy said, sounding annoyed. "What are you saying, Isabel?"

"Well, I think Amber's struggling with this because you're going about it the wrong way," Isabel said.

"Am I?" Kathy asked in a strangely calm voice.

"Yes. I'd like to see her skate her whole program. With the music," Isabel added.

Amber felt every one of her muscles tense. *Nobody* spoke to Kathy that way. Amber saw Kathy's cheeks flush. The coach's mouth tightened, but her tone was extra pleasant.

"I don't think that's a very good idea," Kathy said calmly. "There's really no sense doing the whole program when the parts aren't ready."

Amber looked at the frown on Isabel's face. "But it won't hurt, will it?" Isabel asked. "Maybe Amber just needs to feel all the pieces go together one more time." She looked at Amber and smiled.

Amber swallowed hard. "Uh, I'll do whatever you guys think is best," she said.

"Well, I *am* the sponsor," Isabel said quietly.

Kathy looked at Isabel. She took a deep breath. "All right. Amber, take your starting position." Kathy skated over to the booth next to the ice where the tape player was. Amber skated to center ice.

"I can't wait to see this," Isabel said, clapping her hands in delight.

"Ready?" Kathy called. "I'm starting the tape." Kathy skated to the boards and stood near Isabel.

Amber couldn't help feeling a little nervous as the

opening notes boomed over the sound system. The music was a medley of jazzy Broadway show tunes. Blake Michaels, the choreographer for Silver Blades, had designed quick, precise, yet playful movements to go with the music. Amber thought they really captured her personality as a skater.

Amber had skated the same program to the same music for about six months. She knew it by heart, even if she didn't always hit every move perfectly.

She began the routine, concentrating especially hard on her triple flip–double loop combination and the other triple jumps. The four minutes flew by. Amber came to a stop in front of Isabel and Kathy with a spray of ice chips.

"Well, what do you think?" Amber asked. She felt proud. She had landed every jump perfectly.

"It was—" Isabel began.

"Pretty good," Kathy finished for her. "Except for that footwork sequence." She glanced at Isabel. "It still needs work."

"Yes," Isabel murmured. She seemed distracted.

"Well, time's up for today," Kathy said, glancing at her watch. "I've got a lesson with Nikki and Alex next. See you this afternoon, Amber." Kathy skated to the far end of the rink.

Amber stepped off the ice. She bent to slip on her skate guards and heard Isabel muttering beside her.

"This isn't going to work," Isabel griped. "This won't work at all."

Amber felt her heart sink. She straightened up and

turned to Isabel. "What won't work?" she asked nervously.

"Your program," Isabel said, keeping her voice low so that no one would overhear. "No wonder you have trouble with your footwork. You need much better choreography. And your music—it should be completely different."

Amber felt stunned. "But—I think the choreography is great. Is there really so much wrong with my skating?"

"No, not with your skating," Isabel insisted. "But the presentation doesn't highlight your strengths at all."

"But I've always done well with this program," Amber said quietly. "Everyone at Silver Blades thinks Blake's a great choreographer."

"He may be good, but he's certainly not great," Isabel declared. "What you need, Amber, is someone at the top of the profession. You're going to be a world-class skater. You can't let the people around you hold you back. I'm going to get you a brand-new program."

"Wow. A brand-new program—better than anyone else's in Silver Blades?" Amber said. "Better than Tori's, even?" she blurted out.

"Trust me. You'll blow everyone away," Isabel predicted.

"Great!" Amber said. "I can't wait!"

6

Thunk! Tori was trying to land a double axel. Amber had seen her miss it twice already. She shook her head.

It was Saturday morning, and Amber was standing by the boards watching Tori practice. For some reason, Tori wasn't getting the height she needed on her jumps. She didn't look like herself at all.

"Tori, you look exhausted," Nikki said when Tori skated over toward the group gathered by the boards. "Are you okay?"

"Sure. I'm just tired, that's all," Tori said, brushing ice off her legs. "I can't believe I missed a double axel. I haven't missed that jump in months."

Amber looked at her. "Well, if your jumps aren't going well, I know something you could try," she said slowly.

"No—forget it," Tori said. "I'm not interested in your lucky-routine ideas. I already told you!"

"Okay, okay." Amber held up her hands. "It was just a suggestion."

"Just because it works for all of *us*, don't let that pressure you," Nikki said.

"Uh-huh. And does Alex know about your lucky bracelet?" Tori asked.

"No," Nikki said. "And he doesn't have to."

"Okay, but if you're doing everything well because of your good-luck charms, then what's going to happen when they run out?" Tori asked. "Your old skate lace will break eventually, Nikki. What if you lose your rabbit's foot, Haley? And—"

"Forget it, Tori. You're not going to talk us out of this," Amber said. "We're doing great."

Tori shrugged. "Well, so am I. I mean, I passed the senior test without a good-luck charm, didn't I?"

Amber frowned. Tori was really rubbing it in. Well, maybe she's just tired, Amber told herself. That's why she snapped at me.

"Our good-luck charms *will* wear out someday," Nikki said. "But for now, it's good enough for me."

"What's good enough?"

Amber whirled around and saw Alex standing behind them, an amused expression on his face. Alex was very cute. He was tall, with curly black hair. He was also one of the biggest flirts in Silver Blades.

"And what's this about lucky charms?" he asked.

"Wait—I thought that was a breakfast cereal." He winked at Nikki.

Amber giggled. Alex could be so funny sometimes.

"Everyone here except me is totally into superstition," Tori announced. "Haley has this lucky rabbit's foot—"

"*Eeuw!* Disgusting," Alex commented.

"It's *fake*, okay? I'd never carry a real one," Haley insisted.

"And Amber touches her toes before every jump, and Martina wipes her skate blades," Tori explained. "They're all trying to get me to believe in this lucky-charm stuff. As if it has anything to do with how well I skate!"

"Hmm. I've heard about stuff like that before. Well, what about you?" Alex asked Nikki. "You never told me you had a good-luck charm."

"Nikki's lucky charm is *you*, Alex, didn't you know?" Haley teased, batting her eyelashes.

Amber laughed as Nikki's face turned red with embarrassment. "He is not," Nikki said.

Alex rolled his eyes.

"Seriously, I have this skate lace I've been wearing around my wrist," Nikki confessed. "Ever since the day we landed our star lift for the first time. We haven't missed one since."

"Really?" Alex said. "So what can I say, Tori? I think I'm with them."

"But . . . ," Tori began, looking around at everyone. "Oh, never mind. I give up!" She skated across the ice, away from the group.

"You know what they say," Martina shouted after her. "If you can't beat 'em, join 'em!"

"Never!" Tori called over her shoulder. Then she lifted into a triple flip—and fell right on her rear end again.

Amber looked at Haley. "I think she'll change her mind sooner than she thinks," Amber said.

"You looked terrific in practice today," Isabel said that afternoon. She and Amber were driving downtown, on their way to Violet Knight's.

Violet Knight was a top designer of skating dresses and costumes. Before Isabel had come along, Amber had only dreamed of owning a Knightdress, as they were called. Isabel had taken Amber's measurements the week before and dropped them off at the designer's. Now the dress was ready for Amber to take home.

"You've got such skill, at such a young age. It's really incredible," Isabel went on.

Amber felt herself blush. She got embarrassed whenever Isabel gushed over her. It was almost too much.

"The way things are going, I think you should take the senior test next week," Isabel went on.

"Next week?" Amber practically squealed. "Really?"

"Why not? You're ready," Isabel said, glancing in the rearview mirror.

"But Kathy didn't say anything about scheduling the test," Amber pointed out.

"Kathy knows you're ready," Isabel said. "The sooner you get into seniors, the sooner you can compete in big events. Besides, the ice show auditions are only a week from Monday. Skating as a senior will impress the judges at the audition."

Isabel parked across the street from a pretty Victorian house. A small sign on the lawn said VIOLET KNIGHT—DESIGNER.

"I'm so excited," Amber said, getting out of the car. "I've never been to a real designer before. We usually just buy my skating dresses at the rink shops."

"This is going to make a big difference," Isabel said, setting her car alarm with a remote control.

Amber still couldn't get over what a nice, huge car it was. Of course, she thought, why am I surprised? If she has enough money to spend on me, then she has enough money for any kind of car she wants.

"You're going to have your very own distinctive look, just in time for the audition," Isabel said as they climbed the steps to the house. "No one's going to forget seeing you skate."

Amber smiled as she went inside. "I hope not."

She thought of Nancy Kerrigan's elegant white

dresses in the Olympics and the sparkly blue gypsy outfit Michelle Kwan wore when she won the World Championships. Now Amber could be just like them—thanks to Isabel.

"Hello, I'm Isabel Hart." Isabel greeted the woman at the front desk. "We're here for Amber Armstrong's dress."

"Oh, is this Amber?" The woman looked up with a smile. "Violet finished your dress yesterday. Come on, let's have a look. You can try it on, and we'll make sure it fits properly."

Amber followed Isabel into the back room, where a dozen dresses were hanging on a rack. A few mannequins stood around the room. They looked like blank-faced people with pins sticking out all over.

"Here it is." The woman pulled a dress off the rack and held it out to Amber. "There's a changing room right over there."

Amber ran her hand over the material. The dress was black, with silver sequins trimming the neckline. It had flesh-toned netting at the neck and shoulders.

"It—It's the most beautiful dress I've ever seen!" Amber blurted out.

"And you're going to look beautiful in it," Isabel said with a warm smile. "Now go ahead—try it on."

Amber hurried into the changing room. She quickly slipped out of her sweatshirt, T-shirt, and jeans and pulled the dress up over her shoulders. She straightened it around her hips, then zipped up the back. It fit perfectly. The dress was so glamorous, and so grown-up. She'd never owned a black dress before. Her mom always chose dresses in pastel blues or pinks. Amber felt about ten years older in black.

"Oh, Isabel. I love it!" Amber cried. She stepped out of the dressing room and twirled around. "What do you think?" she asked. "Is it what you wanted?"

"What do *you* think?" Isabel asked.

"It's absolutely perfect!" Amber said. She spun around again, letting the silky fabric swirl around her hips.

"You know what, Amber? In that dress you *look* like a champion," Isabel said.

Amber grinned. She felt like one, too. "I can't wait to get home and show this to my mom," she said.

"So, Mom? What do you think? Isn't it gorgeous?"

Amber's mother was sitting on the sofa in their apartment. She stood up when Amber turned around, modeling the new dress.

"Amber, it's very pretty," Mrs. Armstrong said slowly. "But isn't it a bit . . . old for you?"

"Mom!" Amber cried.

"What?" Mrs. Armstrong replied.

"It's not too old for me," Amber said. "My old dress is way too *young* for me, that's all. It's a good change."

Amber's mother eyed the dress critically. "I don't know, Amber. Are you sure about this?"

"Yes, and so is Isabel, and so is the woman who designed it for me," Amber said. Why was her mother being so difficult?

"Mom, it's *supposed* to make me look older," Amber went on. "After all, I'm going to be a senior skater soon. I have to look like one, especially for my audition." She admired the dress in the mirror near the apartment's front door. "Anyway, you know what Isabel said?"

Mrs. Armstrong looked at Amber. "No, what?"

"She said this makes me look like a champion," Amber said proudly. "And guess what? She says I'm ready to take the senior-level test next week."

"Next week?" Mrs. Armstrong asked, her eyes widening. "Isn't that kind of sudden?"

"Not really," Amber said with a shrug. "I mean, I've been working toward it nonstop for the past couple of weeks. I'm sure I'll pass."

"Well, don't be overconfident," her mother warned.

"I'm not," Amber said. "Isabel says you have to believe in yourself, or you'll never make it all the way. Hey, look what else she got when we were downtown today." Amber ran into her room and came out carrying several bags. She dumped the contents onto the carpet. "A new pair of jeans, and this sweater, and some shoes . . ."

"Isabel bought all that for you?" Mrs. Armstrong sounded worried. "Why?"

"I don't know," Amber said, unfolding the blue sweater and holding it up against her. "She wanted to, I guess. Isn't this sweater pretty?"

"Yes, but you're not going to keep it," her mother said firmly. "You've got to return all of those."

"*Return* them? But Mom, why?" Amber asked.

"Because. It's one thing for Isabel to buy you a new skating dress. But purchasing a whole new wardrobe for you?" Mrs. Armstrong shook her head. "No, that's not her job."

"But she's my sponsor," Amber argued. "Sponsors do stuff like that."

"She's your sponsor as far as skating is concerned, and that's it," her mother said. "It's not her responsibility to buy everything in the world for you."

"But it's only a pair of jeans and a sweater—" Amber began.

"Amber, don't argue with me. You know returning the clothes to Isabel is the right thing to do. Promise me you'll give them back the next time you see her," Mrs. Armstrong said, staring into Amber's eyes.

"Okay, if I have to," Amber told her mother. "Though I still don't understand what's wrong with keeping them," she added under her breath.

"Good. Then that's settled," Mrs. Armstrong said. "Now how about changing into something less formal," she joked, "and we'll have some dinner."

"Sure, " Amber said. She stuffed the new clothes back into the bags and walked off toward her bedroom. She couldn't believe her mother was making such a fuss about a few new clothes. She dropped the bags on her bed with a sigh.

How could she just give them back? It might hurt Isabel's feelings.

Amber had a terrible thought. What if Isabel became so hurt—or angry—that she decided not to sponsor Amber after all?

No, Isabel would never do that to me, Amber told herself. But still . . . she's done so much for me already. I'd hate to have her think I was ungrateful.

There was only one thing to do. Amber carefully packed the new clothes in the bottom of her skate bag. She'd just take them to the rink and keep them in her locker. Maybe her mother would change her mind.

7

"Try the footwork sequence again, Amber," Kathy said. It was Monday morning practice. "I'm not sure that was as clean as you need it to be."

"What are you talking about? It was squeaky clean," Isabel said.

Kathy slowly turned to face her. Isabel had been interfering more and more in practice lately. Kathy took a deep breath before speaking.

"Even if it was perfect, why shouldn't Amber run through it again, just to make sure?" Kathy asked.

"Because," Isabel argued, "why bother? She's perfectly solid. No one in their right mind would fail her on the senior-level test tomorrow."

Amber smiled. Finally, it was really going to happen—tomorrow! *If* Isabel was right. But if Kathy was right . . .

"Maybe I *should* do it one more time," she said nervously.

"No, you don't need to," Isabel said. "I've seen it a hundred times now. Ninety-nine out of a hundred times you're right on the money, Amber. I'd rather see you cut your practice a little short today and rest up for your big day tomorrow."

Amber glanced at Kathy, who was staring at Isabel. Kathy's face was turning pink. She wore the same expression she had when someone was late to practice.

"I still think it's a good idea to be more than ready," Kathy said evenly. "That way there's no room for error."

"Well, let's ask Amber. Amber, don't you feel ready?" Isabel said, turning to her with a smile.

Amber grinned back. "Sure. I can't wait."

"Then it's settled," Isabel declared. "We quit for today, and we'll all see each other tomorrow at the test."

"Well, of course—" Kathy began.

"Of course what?" Amber asked quickly.

"Well, I mean, maybe you're ready, and maybe you're not," Kathy said. "But in either case, the worst thing that can happen is that you won't pass. Which is no big deal. You'll just have to take the test again."

Amber felt her pulse quicken. "Take it again?" she said. "If Tori can pass it on her first try, then I can, too. I'm not going to fail." She stared at Kathy and felt tears forming in the corners of her eyes. "How can you be so mean?"

"I'm not being mean," Kathy said sternly. "I'm being realistic. You *could* fail, Amber."

"I could—but I'm not going to!" Amber insisted. "Why don't you believe in me? You're supposed to be my coach."

"I am your coach," Kathy said. "And good coaches don't push their athletes into things unless they're ready." She frowned at Isabel.

"I am ready. I've been ready forever," Amber said. "Maybe if you weren't so negative all the time, you'd see that. Like Isabel does."

"You're certainly not going to fail," Isabel said, putting her arm around Amber's shoulders. "You're going to do great."

Amber looked up at her and smiled. "Thanks." At least *Isabel* believed in her.

"Go ahead, Amber," Kathy said the next afternoon. "They're ready for you."

"Good luck," Isabel said. "You'll be great."

Kathy nodded. "Don't forget to concentrate."

Amber stepped onto the ice. She could hardly believe that the three judges seated near the ice were waiting for *her*. She'd been imagining this moment forever.

Too bad Mom has to be at work, Amber thought.

She'd always pictured her mother being there in the stands when she passed her senior test. Amber grinned. She'd just make sure her mom had tickets when she skated in the Olympics! As Isabel always said, shoot for the stars!

Amber had arrived early to do her lucky spin before the judges arrived. Good thing, too, she thought as she finished the required elements for the test. She hadn't made a single error. She noticed the judges making notes on their clipboards.

"It's time for your freestyle program," Kathy called to her. "Four minutes."

Amber took a deep breath as Kathy handed the music tape to the judges. This moment was so important. If she blew it . . . No, she couldn't let herself think that way. She wouldn't blow it. Everything depended on it.

Amber glided across the ice and took up her starting position. She was glad she was still skating her old program for the test. She knew it so well; she was sure she'd get it right. She just had to.

Amber launched herself into her opening moves. She was really pouring it on for the judges. She wanted them to know how much she deserved to skate at the senior level.

Amber swept into the most difficult move in her program, the triple loop–triple toe loop combination. She'd nailed it in practice, but things could always go wrong on the ice. If they didn't, everyone would be an Olympic medalist.

Amber felt a rush of cool air as she jumped effort-lessly. She landed both jumps cleanly.

I did it, she thought. I did it!

She finished her program with a flourish. She threw her arms up over her head and glanced at the judges and then at Kathy and Isabel. She skated quickly over to the boards. She felt as if she would die of suspense. But the head judge came over to her immediately. "Congratulations, Amber," she said. "You've passed the senior-level test."

"Thank you," Amber said. "Oh, thank you, thank you, thank you!"

Isabel pumped her fist in the air, an ecstatic smile on her face. Amber skated over to Isabel and threw her arms around her. "Thanks, Isabel. I couldn't have done it without you."

Kathy skated over, a wide smile plastered on her face. She flashed Amber the thumbs-up signal. "Con-gratulations, Amber. You were terrific," she said.

"Thanks, Kathy," Amber said.

Kathy glanced at Isabel. She smiled again at Am-ber and glided across the rink.

"Now, there's only one thing we should do," Isabel said. She picked her coat up from the bleachers.

"Win the audition next week," Amber said, nod-ding.

"Well, sure, but not now," Isabel said, laughing. "Now we've got to go out and celebrate. I want to take you to the nicest restaurant in town."

"Really?" Amber asked. "Great! Can I call my

mom? She should be off work in half an hour, and she could meet us."

"I don't know, Amber," Isabel said. "I think it might be better if it was just the two of us."

"Just us?" Amber repeated. "How come?"

"There are lots of things we need to talk about," Isabel said. "I wouldn't want your mother to be bored with all our skating talk, would you?"

"No," Amber said doubtfully. Actually, her mom kept up with every aspect of Amber's skating. She was never bored hearing about it. Mrs. Armstrong had changed her whole life for Amber's skating.

Still, Amber didn't want to seem rude by disagreeing with Isabel. She felt a twinge of guilt but pushed it aside. Isabel was her sponsor, after all. What could be more natural than the two of them having dinner together?

"I thought you said we were going to celebrate," she said finally.

"Sure we are," Isabel said, heading for the door. "But we also have to start planning your *next* victory. You realize you need to start training for your first senior-level Regionals, don't you?"

Amber grinned, following Isabel out the door. *Senior-level Regionals.* The words had never sounded so good to her before. Isabel's enthusiasm made Amber feel unstoppable.

"Okay, I'll go call my mom and tell her I'll be home late," she told Isabel. "Where are we going, anyway?"

"Oh, somewhere nice, expensive, and maybe a little funky . . ." Isabel thought for a minute. "How about the Wildflower Cafe?"

"Cool!" Amber exclaimed. "I've heard kids talking about that restaurant, but I never thought I'd be inside it."

She practically danced off to the pay phone. This must be what Cinderella felt like, she thought. Wow! A fancy dinner at the Wildflower Cafe!

"Amber! Where in the world have you been?" Mrs. Armstrong cried as Amber walked in the front door of their apartment a few hours later.

"You know where I was. Isabel and I had dinner at the Wildflower Cafe," Amber reminded her mother. "I called you from the rink, remember?"

"Yes, but I didn't expect you to be there till nine o'clock," Mrs. Armstrong said. "It's a school night, Amber. You've still got homework to do. And you have to be up at five A.M. for practice tomorrow."

"But Mom—" Amber began.

"But nothing," Mrs. Armstrong said. "You may have a sponsor now, but you still have rules. Do you think Isabel's going to help you in school the same way she can help you on the ice? *I'm* your mother. Not Isabel."

Amber took a few steps back. She'd never seen her mother so upset.

"Why are you so mad at me?" Amber asked, feeling hurt. "You should be congratulating me, Mom. I just passed the senior-level test. But instead of being happy for me, you're mad because someone took me out to dinner."

"Amber, of course I'm happy about the test," Mrs. Armstrong said. "But that doesn't mean you can disobey our rules. Those aren't going to change, no matter what happens to your skating."

Amber scuffed one toe back and forth against the carpet. "What was I supposed to do—tell Isabel she couldn't take me out to dinner?"

"No, but you could have told her that you needed to be home by eight," Mrs. Armstrong said. "She would have understood."

Amber stared at the floor. "I'm sorry I'm so late. I didn't mean for it to be a big deal," she said.

Her mother sighed. "It's all right, just don't do it again." She smiled faintly. "Well. You almost missed the special surprise I made for you. Come into the kitchen."

Amber followed her mother through the living room. "You made something special for me?" she asked. Now she was really starting to feel bad.

"Okay, now close your eyes," Mrs. Armstrong said.

Amber put her hands over her eyes, shutting them tight. A few seconds later, she smelled a match that had just gone out.

"You can open them now," Mrs. Armstrong said cheerfully.

Amber opened her eyes. Her mother was holding out a plate. On it was a cake covered with fluffy white frosting—and the cake was shaped like an ice skate. Candles decorated the top, and Amber's name was spelled out in glittery gold letters.

"Congratulations on making it to seniors." Mrs. Armstrong kissed Amber on the cheek. "I'm very proud of you, and so is your dad."

"Thanks," Amber said. She stared at the cake, feeling guilty. While she had been out with Isabel, her mother had been home alone, creating this surprise. I should have invited her to come with us, Amber thought.

"So what are you waiting for?" Mrs. Armstrong said. "Grab a knife and cut us some dessert."

"Sure, Mom. This looks great," Amber said. She put the cake on the counter and took a knife out of the drawer. She cut two large slices and placed them on two plates.

Smiling, her mother handed her a napkin and a fork. "Let's dig in, sweetheart," she said.

Amber stared at the cake on her plate. She felt awful. No way could she eat this cake. And no way could she tell her mom why—she was too full from her dinner with Isabel.

8

"**S**o, what are you working on today?" Mrs. Armstrong asked as she and Amber stepped off the bus the next morning. Mrs. Armstrong usually stayed to watch Amber at morning practice.

They hurried the few blocks from the bus stop to the Seneca Hills Ice Arena.

"I don't know what we'll work on now," Amber said. She shifted the skate bag on her shoulder. She tilted her head and grinned at her mother. "Senior stuff, I guess." She laughed.

"Maybe Kathy will teach you how to accept the gold medal," Mrs. Armstrong teased.

"I already know how to do that," Amber said. She curtsied, then leaned down as if a judge were placing a ribbon around her neck.

Mrs. Armstrong pinched her lightly on the back of her neck. "Okay, you can wake up now."

"No fair. I was just getting ready for my television interview," Amber protested. The two of them walked into the ice rink arm in arm, giggling.

Isabel was waiting at the front entrance. "Oh, Amber. There you are!" she exclaimed.

"Of course I'm here," Amber said. "I'm not late, am I?"

"No, not at all," Isabel said. "But sometimes I worry about you taking the bus. Maybe I should start picking you up in the mornings."

"That won't be necessary," Mrs. Armstrong said. "I always make sure Amber gets here on time."

Isabel smiled. "And I appreciate it. But it's such a lot of time out of your schedule, isn't it? Bringing Amber down here, then taking another bus to get to work?"

"It's no trouble, really. I'm used to it. And I look forward to watching Amber's practice sessions."

Isabel frowned, picking a piece of lint off the cuff of her coat sleeve. "I'm sure you have a million other things to do. Don't you get bored?"

"Bored?" Amber echoed, laughing. "Mom's been watching me skate forever. She probably knows more than most people about what I'm supposed to be doing out there."

"Well, we're going to be working on some new things today," Isabel told Mrs. Armstrong. "It might be awfully slow. And I'm going to need Amber's total concentration."

"*You'll* need it? But Kathy is Amber's coach," Mrs. Armstrong said. "Isn't she?"

"Of course she is," Isabel said. "But we're both helping Amber."

"Isabel kind of helps Kathy now," Amber tried to explain.

"Oh, really. And you've also started deciding who can watch Amber practice?" Mrs. Armstrong asked, a sharp note creeping into her voice.

"Actually, I think I should be the only one who watches her," Isabel replied, gazing at Mrs. Armstrong. "That usually works best."

"I've been watching Amber practice for years. I make special arrangements to see that I can do just that," Amber's mother said, sounding offended. "Our family's gone to a lot of trouble so Amber can skate here, and I enjoy watching her. She's my daughter, and I'm very proud of her. I'm certainly not leaving," Mrs. Armstrong said coldly, "whether you like it or not."

She marched toward the bleachers, leaving Isabel and Amber standing in the lobby.

"Well." Isabel rubbed her hands together. Her cheeks were very pink, and her lower lip trembled. "I'm sorry your mother and I couldn't see eye to eye. I'm going to get a cup of coffee. Why don't you get changed, Amber dear."

Amber nodded. "I'll be right out."

Isabel marched down the hall toward the snack bar. As soon as she was gone, Amber hurried to the bleachers to see her mother.

"Don't mind Isabel, Mom. She's just in a bad mood," Amber said quickly. "I'm sure she doesn't really want you to leave."

"Yes, she does," Mrs. Armstrong said. "But you know what? That's not for her to decide. She can't control our lives. I've always watched you practice, Amber. I'm not about to stop now."

"Don't get upset, Mom. Please," Amber said. "Isabel knows what she's doing. She really does. She's going to make me a winner."

"We'll see," Mrs. Armstrong told her.

Amber hurried into the locker room. She threw on her practice clothes, then returned to the rink for her off-ice warm-up. Finally she skated around the ice and did a few more stretches. Kathy glided onto the ice to begin the lesson.

"Should we start by seeing your winning senior-test program again?" Kathy teased.

"Well, I don't know if I can do it *that* well again," Amber joked. She was relieved to see Kathy in a good mood. At least so far. Amber could imagine how intense the training might get from now on. She could just hear Kathy saying, "You can go back to juniors if you're going to skate like that."

"Nonsense!" Isabel's voice rang out across the

rink. Isabel strode over to them. "Of course Amber could skate that well again. But the point is, she doesn't want to."

"I don't?" Amber asked. She glanced at Kathy, then back at Isabel. "Why not?"

"You're a senior-level skater now, remember?" Isabel said.

"Of course she remembers," Kathy said. "What does that have to do with anything?" She glanced at her watch. "We really should get going."

Isabel held up her hand. "Please, Kathy. I have something to say first."

Kathy looked at Isabel as if Isabel had said she wanted to fly to the moon and back before Amber's lesson. "Yes?" she asked, her voice barely polite.

"I've been thinking about Amber's program. Quite a bit, actually," Isabel began.

"*Have* you?" Kathy said frostily.

"Yes. And what I've been thinking is now that she's in seniors, her music just won't cut it," Isabel said. "I mean, skating to Broadway show tunes is fine for a junior skater. But when you move into the senior level—"

"I know quite a bit about what's done at senior level," Kathy interrupted.

"Of course you do," Isabel went on. "But my point is simply that Amber's more grown-up now. Her program needs to grow up, too. That's why I've taken the liberty of choosing new music for her, in time for the audition next Monday."

Isabel hurried over to the Plexiglas booth. "Now, if I can just find the tape, I'll pop it in and you two can listen—"

"Wait a second," Kathy said. "We haven't discussed creating a new program for Amber."

"Well, it makes sense, doesn't it? New level, new program," Isabel said.

Amber glanced uneasily at Kathy. "I could have a new program," she said. "Or I could stick with my old one. Really, either way is fine with me."

Loud orchestral music boomed out of the speakers. Mournful violins competed against a thunderous bass drum. The melody sounded strange to Amber. She could barely find a tune. *Is this music really for me?* Amber wondered.

She glanced at her mother up in the bleachers. *What does Mom think of all this?*

The music finished with a clang of cymbals. Isabel turned to Amber with a smile. "Well, what do you think? Dramatic, isn't it?"

Amber smiled uneasily. "I guess so," she said. She felt torn. She wanted to be honest, but she owed so much to Isabel. She didn't want to trash the new music Isabel had picked.

"It's kind of weird in some parts," Amber said, biting her lip.

"It's very sophisticated music," Isabel said, smiling.

"Are you serious?" Kathy asked. "*That* is what you want Amber to skate to? That dark, brooding piece?"

"It's not brooding. It's serious, powerful, and full of emotion," Isabel answered.

"Amber's not that kind of skater at all," Kathy said. "She's light, she's young. This won't show off her best qualities; it'll bury them. She can't pull off a routine to music like that."

"I'm not *that* young," Amber protested.

"And she'll grow into it," Isabel insisted. "Amber can be whatever kind of skater she wants to be. I think this is the direction she should be moving in. The sooner, the better."

Amber was thoughtful. "If it's time for my program to get more serious, that's okay with me," she said.

"Well, it's not okay with me," Kathy said.

"Give it a chance," Isabel told her. "Wait until you see the new program I've sketched out. I've hired a new choreographer, someone I know from New York, to help design it."

"You've what?" Kathy said.

"You'll love him. He's worked with some of the best new skaters," Isabel went on, ignoring Kathy's interruption. "Blake's very nice, and he's perfectly competent. But he really can't help Amber right now. So Blake is out, and Philippe is in. It's all been arranged. All I need to do is let Blake know his services are no longer needed and—"

"Wait a second," Kathy said. "Hold on, Isabel. You're firing Blake?"

"Amber can't have two choreographers," Isabel

said. "And Philippe is clearly the talent here. Amber, you're going to love working with him."

"I—I am?" Amber stammered. Suddenly it felt as if things were moving awfully fast.

"No, she's not," Kathy said. "Since when do you call the shots around here, Isabel? As long as I'm coaching Amber, she works—*we* work—with Blake. And she doesn't skate to music that sounds like it belongs in a horror movie."

"Fine," Isabel said. "There's an easy solution to all these problems."

Amber sighed. "That's good," she murmured.

"Right," Kathy said. "We'll keep the Broadway music. Maybe we can make the program a little more sophisticated—"

"No," Isabel said. "You misunderstood me. If you won't work with Philippe, then Amber is no longer training with you."

"What do you mean, Amber is no longer training with me?" Kathy asked, bewildered.

"Must I spell it out for you?" Isabel said. "Consider yourself fired. In the meantime, I'll take over."

Amber's mouth dropped open.

"You can't fire me!" Kathy stared at Isabel in disbelief.

"Of course I can," Isabel said calmly. "I can do whatever's best for Amber. And I think this is best."

Amber couldn't believe what she was hearing. Kathy was fired? This was terrible! Kathy was tough, but Amber respected her. Kathy had stuck with her through thick and thin. Amber couldn't imagine going on without her.

Kathy glared at Isabel. "Well, Isabel, you made it clear from the beginning that you think you can do a better job than me. I guess this is your chance to prove it. Good luck!"

Kathy stormed off the ice. She headed straight for her office. They heard the door slam shut.

Amber blinked in surprise. She had expected Kathy to put up a fight. But Kathy had given in so easily. Maybe Isabel was the only one who really cared about Amber's career, after all.

Isabel turned to Amber. "Would you like to listen to the music again? I can show you some of the new moves I'm thinking of," she suggested. Her voice was calm and steady, as if nothing had happened.

Amber swallowed, thinking quickly. Kathy was a great coach, and Amber owed her a lot. But Isabel was her sponsor, and Isabel could pay for more ice time with any coach. Amber could replace Kathy. But she couldn't replace Isabel.

Amber made up her mind. "Sure," she said. "Let me get used to the music. I'll try whatever moves you want."

9

"**E**arth to Amber!"

Amber looked up, startled to find Martina and Tori standing in front of her. Martina waved her hands in Amber's face.

"Oh—hi," Amber said. She was early for her Wednesday afternoon lesson and had glided onto the ice to do her warm-up. The rink was crowded with kids from Silver Blades. Amber had found a patch of ice near the far end and tried to focus on her skating. But she had started thinking about Kathy. It was hard to believe that Kathy wouldn't teach her this afternoon. Isabel would.

"What's with you, Amber?" Martina asked. "I called your name three times. You are totally out of it."

"Oh, I was just thinking about something," Amber said. "Actually, it's—uh . . ." She broke off and stared blankly across the rink. She didn't know how to explain what had happened with Kathy that morning.

"It's what?" Martina asked. "Amber, you're acting like a total space cadet."

"Um, it's this new program I'm working on," Amber said slowly.

"A new program? Awesome!" Martina said.

"Impossible is more like it," Amber said. "I can't believe Isabel thinks I can learn a new program in one week. And my new music is—"

"New music? You have a new program *and* new music?" Tori interrupted. "Why?"

"Isabel felt like I needed a change, especially with the ice show auditions coming up. This program's more mature. And a lot more . . . complicated," Amber explained.

"They all seem complicated at first," Martina said, nodding in agreement. "Then you get so sick of them you feel like you could do every move in your sleep."

"Just do your lucky routine before you try it, Amber." Tori giggled. "I guarantee you'll do well."

"Very funny," Amber said sarcastically.

"Well, I don't think it's funny," Martina replied. "How does your lucky routine go again? I might need it myself sometime."

"What's the matter—is yours wearing out?" Tori scoffed.

"No, but I'd like to have an extra one. You know, a backup," Martina said.

"You've got to be kidding!" Tori rolled her eyes in disbelief.

"Nope," Martina said. "So let's see it, Amber. We shared our lucky charms with you."

"Okay. It's really easy. Watch." Amber demonstrated her ritual. She touched her toes, spun around, then stretched her arms above her head.

"The Armstrong spin." Martina copied her moves. "It's a great move. It could become as famous as a lutz someday."

Tori pushed past them. "There's no such thing as a lucky routine," she declared. "And I'm going to prove it. I'll show you right now that superstitions are just plain silly."

Tori skated off. She built up speed and launched herself into a triple toe loop. She spun gracefully in the air but two-footed the landing.

"Rats!" Tori exclaimed. "I've been doing that all week."

Nikki skated up to them. "I saw that, Tori. What were you doing? Your no-luck routine?" She giggled.

"Or the totally-out-of-luck routine?" Martina added.

Amber stifled a giggle as Tori glared at all of them.

"But now I'll try the same jump, doing the Armstrong spin," Tori said. "You'll see—it won't make any difference. I don't even know why I'm wasting my time."

Tori brushed ice shavings off her deep blue skating skirt. She bent down, touched her toes, spun around slowly, and stretched her arms over her head. She looked at Amber, Martina, and Nikki with raised eyebrows. "We'll see how well your lucky charm works now."

Tori circled the rink, then headed back toward the group. When she was right in front of everybody, she lifted into another triple toe loop. She completed her rotations and landed the jump on one foot.

"That was perfect!" Amber cried. She gaped at Tori.

Nikki and Martina stared, their jaws hanging. "She did it," Nikki said. "She really did it."

"Way to go, Tori!" Martina shouted.

Tori stared at the ice and then at her skates in total disbelief. "I don't believe it! Did that actually work?" She turned to Amber. "I don't believe it. What did you do?"

"*I* didn't do anything," Amber said. "But *you* landed a perfect triple toe loop. That was fantastic."

"All right, I'm trying this again," Tori said. "One time doesn't prove anything."

Tori did the Armstrong spin again. Then she circled the rink, gathered speed—and performed another perfect triple toe loop.

Tori skated slowly up to Amber, Martina, and Nikki. "Well," she said. "I guess I'll be using your lucky routine now, too."

"Great," Amber began. "But next time, you should make sure you touch each skate with the opposite index finger and—"

"Amber!" Haley's voice rang out angrily across the rink. She hurried over from the locker room. "What exactly do you think you're doing?" she demanded.

"I'm showing Tori my good-luck routine," Amber replied. "What's wrong, Haley?"

Haley glared at her. Amber had never seen her look so mad before. "You know what's wrong. I'm talking about Kathy," Haley said. "I'm talking about what you did to her. She was just in the weight room with me and she told me all about it."

"All about what?" Martina asked.

"What's going on?" Nikki wanted to know.

Tori eyed Amber in surprise. "What did you do to Kathy?"

"Nothing," Amber said. "I didn't do anything."

"She fired Kathy," Haley told everyone. "*Isabel's* going to be her coach now. And she fired Blake, too. She's getting a new choreographer—some guy from New York. Blake and Kathy aren't good enough for her anymore."

"Wait a second," Amber said. "It wasn't like that at all."

"You fired Kathy? Kathy Bart? And Blake?" Nikki asked. "I can't believe it."

Martina's eyes widened. "But Amber, Kathy's a great coach. She just helped you get into the senior levels. Why would you fire her?"

Amber felt a wave of helplessness. "Because, I . . . it's because, well, Isabel's paying my way now, and—"

"And you think you're too good for Kathy and Blake now. Just because you have some rich sponsor." Tori shook her head in disgust. "I suppose you think you're better than the rest of us now. Is that it?"

"No, of course not," Amber protested. "I don't think that at all. Isabel really wants to help me, that's all. And she and Kathy just didn't agree on stuff."

"As if you could do better than Kathy!" Haley cried. "Isabel's not even a real coach."

"Yes, she is," Amber argued. "She was a skater once, too. She knows a lot."

"I can't believe it," Martina muttered. "It seems so weird."

"Other skaters change coaches all the time," Amber said. "You guys know that. And anyway, *I* didn't get rid of Kathy. Isabel did."

"So, do you just go along with whatever Isabel says and does?" Haley asked.

"No—you guys have it all wrong," Amber said. "I'd be nowhere without Isabel." Her voice came out a lot louder than she'd meant it to.

Tori stared at her. "You got plenty far before you

even met Isabel. Don't forget, you've only known her for a couple of weeks."

"But I can go even further now," Amber said. "Isabel can pay for extra lessons, more ice time, new skating dresses—everything. And if she wants to make changes, then I'm going to let her."

"You can't let her run your whole life," Tori insisted. "That's ridiculous."

"Of course you don't understand, Tori," Amber said fiercely. "You've always had everything you've ever wanted. But you know what? Before Isabel, I couldn't afford even *half* as much ice time as you. I had *one* good outfit to wear for competitions. What do you know about being poor? Nothing!"

"That's not fair," Nikki began to protest.

"You don't have to be rich to be a good skater," Martina said flatly. "My family sure isn't rich."

Amber shook her head. "You still don't understand. I would have been stuck at the junior level forever if Isabel hadn't come along. It would have taken me months and months to get in enough practice time to pass the senior test. With Isabel, I did it in a few weeks. I owe everything to her."

"Listen, everyone," Nikki said. "Let's all calm down. We—"

"Amber!" Isabel's voice called across the rink. Amber turned and saw Isabel striding toward the boards nearby. "I need to give you some changes to your new program," Isabel said. "Philippe just faxed them to me."

"Who's Philippe?" Haley asked.

"Amber's new choreographer," Isabel told her. "He's from New York. He's too busy this week to fly up and work on the program. But I'm sure he'll be here next week."

"Excuse *me*," Haley muttered. She raised her eyebrows and exchanged looks with Martina, Nikki, and Tori. They glided to the other end of the ice together.

Isabel frowned. "What was that all about?" she asked, looking after the group. "They seemed . . . almost rude."

"Don't mind them. We were sort of arguing about something," Amber said. "They were kind of upset about Kathy not being my coach anymore and all that."

"Oh." Isabel nodded. "Well, of course. They're jealous."

"Jealous?" Amber repeated.

"Sure. A lot of exciting things are about to happen to you. Now that I'm here, your career is really going to take off. My advice? Get used to it." Isabel shook her head. "A lot of girls are going to be jealous of you from now on." She reached over and ruffled Amber's hair. "And who wouldn't be?"

"But I don't want them to be jealous of me. I want them to be my friends," Amber said. "This is so frustrating."

"I know. But sometimes friends don't understand," Isabel said. "And if it comes to a choice between them and skating, well . . ."

Amber stared at Isabel. "I guess there *is* no choice," Amber finally said. "Skating is more important than anything—or anyone."

10

Isabel blew the whistle hanging around her neck. "Amber, not again! You were supposed to do a flying camel there, not a spiral," she shouted. "Feel the music!"

Amber frowned, stopping for what felt like the hundredth time during her Friday lesson. "How can I *feel* the music when I don't even *like* the music?" she asked.

"Listen harder. You'll learn to like it in time," Isabel said.

"Yeah, right. How *much* time?" Amber replied under her breath.

Isabel had been yelling at her for the past hour. As hard as Amber tried, she just couldn't remember her new program.

"Maybe this would be easier if Kathy were here," Amber suggested. "Kathy would—"

"Forget Kathy," Isabel said. "It's you and me now. Just start again." Isabel punched the tape player, and Amber's new music blared. "And this time, remember what I said about rhythm," Isabel added.

"This music doesn't have any rhythm," Amber complained. "Those drumbeats make no sense to me. Maybe we could pick out some different music. Maybe Philippe knows some better music I could use."

"Philippe is the one who chose this music," Isabel said. "It will work, Amber. Just concentrate. Come on, now. Let's see that champion spirit."

"Okay, okay." Amber began the program again. She circled the ice with her arms outstretched as she gathered speed. She dug her toe pick into the ice and leaped into her first jump, a triple flip. She landed it cleanly.

"Well done!" Isabel called. "That was crisp and polished."

Amber came out of her next jump combination and moved into a set of backward crossovers. Okay, she thought. Now I do the . . .

She felt a burst of panic. She couldn't remember what she was supposed to do next. The flying camel, she thought quickly. That must be it. Or was it the . . . Confused, she came to a complete stop.

"No, no, no!" Isabel cried in dismay. "Oh, I'm going to have to talk to Philippe about this. He's got to make this program work better. If it's this hard for you to remember, it has problems."

She snapped off the music. "But Amber, even if Philippe makes some adjustments, you're still going to have to learn this program. And as soon as possible. Your audition's next week."

"Couldn't I just use my old program for the audition?" Amber asked. "I know it backwards and forwards."

"Absolutely not. This is your new look." Isabel shook her head. "There's no time like the present to get rid of your old program," she added firmly. "You're a senior skater now and your program should reflect that. The sooner you learn this routine, the better."

"When can I learn it?" Amber complained. "I'm working every morning and afternoon. But I have school all day. There just isn't time to get a whole new program ready."

"Maybe you should have skipped school for a few days," Isabel said. She smiled at Amber. "You know, many serious skaters end up with tutors."

"But Isabel, I like going to school," Amber said. "It's the only time I get to be with kids my age. I mean, my friends at the rink are all older than me, and I—"

"Never mind," Isabel interrupted. "We'll think about that in the future. For right now, you're still in school."

"Good," Amber said, relieved.

"We'll just have to find another way to schedule extra practices," Isabel said, consulting a small pocket calendar. "In the meantime, I'll see you back here tomorrow at six A.M."

"Six o'clock?" Amber asked. "But—it's Saturday."

"So?" Isabel said, raising her eyebrows.

"Well, uh, we usually don't have to be here so early on Saturdays," Amber said.

"That was the only private ice time I could get," Isabel said.

"Okay," Amber said. She glanced at the clock on the wall. "Yikes! I'd better go change, fast. I'm going shopping with my mom. She might be waiting for me already."

"Go along, then," Isabel said.

"Bye, Isabel," Amber called. "See you tomorrow."

Amber headed toward the locker room. Think about winning that role in the ice show, she told herself. That will be so awesome. And then everyone will see why Isabel is a great sponsor.

Amber turned a corner—and almost ran into Kathy, who was going the other way. Each took a step back. Amber didn't know what to say. She felt her cheeks flush. She dropped her eyes, about to walk right past Kathy.

"Good luck at the audition Monday," Kathy suddenly said. "I'll be rooting for you."

Amber blinked at her, surprised that Kathy was being so nice. She had thought Kathy was mad at her.

"Thanks," she muttered. She and Kathy stood silently for a moment. Then Kathy hurried past to her office. Amber rushed into the locker room.

Amber threw on her clothes in record time. As she dashed out of the locker room she heard Isabel call out.

"Amber! Do you have a second?" Isabel asked.

"Well, my mom—" Amber began.

"This is more important than shopping," Isabel interrupted. "Trust me. I won't keep you long." She took Amber's arm and turned her back toward the rink. Amber saw Tori on center ice, in the middle of a private lesson with Dan Trapp.

Isabel led Amber to a seat in the bleachers. She patted the bench beside her. "Have a seat. There's something we need to talk about."

"But I really should get going," Amber said.

"Just for a few minutes," Isabel pleaded.

Amber sighed and sat down. She watched as Tori landed a triple flip followed by a double axel.

"Tori's definitely ready for the auditions. She looks really good today," Amber commented.

"Yes, she does," Isabel agreed. "She's hitting all her jumps." They watched Tori do a perfect flying sit spin.

"Looks like my lucky routine's working better for her than for me," Amber muttered.

"Pardon me?" Isabel asked.

"Never mind," Amber said. "It's not important."

Isabel stared into Amber's eyes. "Tori is skating

well now," she said. "But *you're* going to win the role on Monday. If you really want to, that is."

Amber nodded. "I do. Of course I do."

"Good. Because I've been thinking," Isabel began, "maybe what we need to do is take you out of Silver Blades."

"Wh—What?" Amber asked, horrified. "But Isabel, why?"

"There aren't very many advantages to being in Silver Blades," Isabel told her. "You can hire your own coach, and ice time, at any rink you like."

"But I love Silver Blades. I don't want to quit—ever!" Amber cried.

"My goodness, Amber, calm down!" Isabel stared at her. "Forget I mentioned it. I can see it's upsetting you. And that's the *last* thing we want."

"I don't want to drop out, ever. I *won't*," Amber insisted.

"Okay! I told you, it's forgotten," Isabel said.

Amber watched Tori skating. Tori really looked great. Amber felt her heart sink. She still hadn't memorized her new program. And it wasn't likely she *could* memorize it before Monday. All of a sudden she didn't feel very good about all the changes that were going on.

"Isabel? Do you really think I can get that program down by Monday?" she asked. "It's Friday already and—"

"Don't worry," Isabel said with assurance. "Of course you can, and you will—with my help. I'll make sure you win that role on Monday. I'll do whatever I can to help. But only if you're as committed as I am."

"Of course I am," Amber said. "It's a huge honor to skate in the Winter Welcome. I'd do anything to be in the show."

"Anything? No matter what?" Isabel asked.

"Yes," Amber said. "Winning is all that matters."

"Good." Isabel patted her on the back. "That's just what I wanted to hear."

Amber stood up as if to leave.

"Wait," Isabel said. "I haven't mentioned the most important thing yet."

Amber sat back down.

Isabel frowned. "It's about our practice tomorrow morning. It's got to be private if we want to make any real progress. I don't want anything distracting you. And that means no guests."

"Sure, okay," Amber said.

"I mean, no one at all," Isabel went on. "I think you understand."

"Do you mean my mom?" Amber asked, biting her lip.

"Exactly. Not even your mom can watch," Isabel replied. "The last time she watched your practice, I saw you look her way several times. We can't afford that kind of distraction. I need your total attention."

"But—" Amber began to protest. Isabel shot her a cold look.

Okay," Amber agreed. "If you say so." She stood

up to leave, and this time Isabel didn't make a move to stop her. Amber hurried out of the rink. Her mom almost always came to practice. How could she tell her not to come? She knew her mother wouldn't be happy about it. Not at all.

I'll just have to make her understand, Amber thought. I'll have to make her see that Isabel only wants the best for me.

And that's what I want, too. Right?

11

Amber stared out the bus window at the pouring rain. She'd never seen such a miserable Saturday morning. And she still hadn't said that her mom couldn't come and watch her practice.

Amber sighed. Over breakfast, she'd hinted at least a dozen times that she wanted to go alone.

"But I won't see you this weekend, between practice and Tiffany's sleepover tonight," her mother said at last.

The sleepover! Amber had nearly forgotten about it. Tiffany's mom was picking her up that afternoon at one o'clock. Amber couldn't wait. Her friends in Silver Blades were barely speaking to her. They all felt she had betrayed Kathy. Amber was dying to hang out with Tiffany. It would be a welcome break from spending all her time with Isabel.

Besides, Amber thought, it will help me relax before the big audition on Monday.

Amber sighed and traced a circle on the steamed-up window with her finger.

"Amber, are you feeling all right?" Mrs. Armstrong put her palm against Amber's forehead.

"I'm *fine*, Mom. I'm just thinking, that's all," Amber said, brushing her mother's hand away.

"Thinking about what?" Mrs. Armstrong asked. "You've been acting funny all morning." She yawned.

"I told you, I have to have my new program down cold before the audition," Amber said.

Mrs. Armstrong frowned. "But the audition is Monday. That's impossible. What can Isabel be thinking?"

"Isabel said I can do it," Amber replied. "But that's why I need to have an extra-good practice today."

The bus turned a corner, heading down the street toward the ice arena. Amber stood up and picked up her skate bag. "Well, see you later, Mom."

"See you later? What do you mean?" Mrs. Armstrong stood up, too. "I'm coming to practice with you, remember?"

"Mom," Amber said. "You—You can't."

Mrs. Armstrong laughed. "Look, Amber, I know your program's not ready yet, and you probably want it to be better before anyone else sees it, but honey—"

"That's not it," Amber said. "It's just that Isabel doesn't want me to have any distractions right now."

"Oh. So I'm a distraction now. That's funny—I thought I was your mother." Mrs. Armstrong's face was turning pink. "Really, Amber. This is going too far. Isabel doesn't have the right to tell me I can't watch my own daughter practice."

"But Mom, she just wants to help me," Amber argued. "I told you, I need to work extra hard today."

Mrs. Armstrong frowned. "You work hard every day, whether I'm there or not."

"But it's different when you're there," Amber said. "I wonder what you're thinking, and I look at you, and—Mom, I just can't afford to waste any time right now. There's almost no time left before the auditions on Monday, and winning that role means *everything* to me." Amber felt tears sting her eyes. She looked around quickly at the people on the bus, aware that she had spoken too loudly. She felt as if everyone was staring at her.

"It means everything to *you*?" Mrs. Armstrong retorted. "Or it means everything to Isabel? Because it seems to me that you're doing everything *she* says, whether you want to or not."

Amber felt her face getting hot. She glanced out the window. Her stop was coming up. She couldn't wait to get off this dumb bus—and away from her mother.

Mrs. Armstrong shook her head. "I don't like the way you've been acting since Isabel came along," she said.

"You know what, Mom? The only reason you don't
like Isabel is because you're jealous of her," Amber
said bluntly. "You're mad because she's the one who
can help me now—not you." As soon as the words
were out of her mouth, Amber regretted saying them.
But she couldn't take them back. It was too late.

Mrs. Armstrong stared at her. "I'm not jealous of
Isabel. I'm glad she can help with your skating. But
that doesn't give her the right to tell me what to do.
And that's why I'm coming to your practice, whether
she thinks it's a good idea or not."

"You're not coming, Mom," Amber shouted. "How
many times do I have to tell you? Isabel doesn't want
you there—and neither do I!"

She ran down the aisle of the bus and yanked the
cord to signal the driver to stop. The doors opened
and Amber flew down the steps and out onto the side-
walk. The day sure was off to a rotten start. She
hoped a good practice would make up for it.

She raced into the arena without looking back. She
charged into the locker room and changed into her
practice clothes. Then she rushed out to the rink. Her
heart was pounding so hard she felt as if she couldn't
breathe.

She quickly performed her warm-up routine. "Amber! Good morning," Isabel called.

Amber glanced up to see Isabel hurrying toward
the ice.

"You're right on time. Good," Isabel said. "Let's
get to work."

Amber scanned the rink. "Where's Philippe? Wasn't he supposed to fly in from New York to work with us today? It's our last chance, you know."

Isabel's face colored. "I know, but he just couldn't make it. Maybe Philippe wasn't the best choice for choreographer," she admitted. "I mean, his work is superb. But I am a bit insulted that he couldn't find time for us in his schedule."

Amber stared at Isabel. "He's *never* coming to help us, is he?" she asked.

Isabel squared her shoulders. "Let's not think about that now," she said. "We have barely enough time as it is. Begin your new program, from the beginning," she ordered. "Let's see how far you can get before you make a mistake."

Amber hesitated. She wasn't sure she understood the moves Philippe had designed. But there was nothing she could do about that now.

She glided onto the ice to take her opening position. She glanced around the rink again. She half expected to see her mother there. She hoped her mom wasn't too mad at her.

Amber shook her head and tried to remember all the things Isabel had told her the day before. The music began. Amber winced. She really hated this music. She raised her arms and moved them over her head, performing the new opening steps.

"No, no, no!" Isabel cried. "Amber, that's all wrong. Do it again," she instructed.

Amber came to an abrupt stop. "But Isabel, I feel

silly waving my arms around. Are you sure this is what Philippe wanted?"

"I'm sure," Isabel said. "It might feel silly, but it doesn't look that way. It looks . . . artistic. Or it will when you get it right."

Amber took a few deep breaths and started over. The music began, and she thrust her arms out, pretending she was tossing flowers.

"Wonderful! That's more like it!" Isabel cried.

Amber launched herself into a quick triple flip.

"Oh—but no," Isabel shouted. "That ruins everything!"

Amber stopped and stared at Isabel. "There wasn't anything wrong with that jump," she said. "I've done it a hundred times."

"But it didn't flow," Isabel told her. "You've got to move from the dramatic arm movements into the jump slowly. Make it elegant, dear."

"I can't slow down going into a jump," Amber argued. "I'll fall flat on my face."

"No, you won't," Isabel said. "You'll have plenty of speed if you ease into it."

"I can't," Amber protested. "And even if I could, who wants to watch jumps that look like they're in slow motion?"

Isabel shook her head impatiently. "It won't be that way on every jump. It's just this one triple flip."

"Maybe I could do a double," Amber suggested. "It might work better with the slower pace."

"Oh, no. Then you won't have the degree of difficulty you need in this program," Isabel replied.

Amber was beginning to lose patience. "Then how about putting in a different move before the double?" she asked. "It could be like a change of pace, and then—"

"Amber, please! Leave the choreography up to me and Philippe. You just worry about your skating," Isabel said.

"I *am* worrying about it," Amber muttered as she took her starting position all over again. "I'm worrying more than I've ever worried before in my whole life!"

The lesson finally ended. Isabel shook her head in disappointment and left the rink. Amber pretended not to see. She turned and found Tori, Nikki, Haley, and Martina right in front of her. They were getting ready for the Silver Blades practice. Not one of them looked at Amber or said hello.

"Uh, hi, you guys," Amber said.

Four blank faces turned toward her. Amber swallowed hard. "That was the most awful lesson of my entire life," she muttered.

"What did you expect? Isabel isn't a real skating coach, not like Kathy," Tori replied.

Amber bit her lip. "It's not Isabel," she said in a small voice. "It's my new program. It's terrible. And I'm terrible at skating it."

She waited for someone to say something to make

her feel better. But nobody said a word. They were still too mad at her.

"Listen, you guys," Amber tried again. "I need to apologize to you about something. Having a sponsor is important to me. I was really excited about having Isabel take care of all my problems. But now I realize how many *new* problems she's caused."

"Really?" Tori said in a cold voice.

"Really," Amber said. "Nothing is more important to me than my friends. I'm so sorry about letting Isabel fire Kathy and Blake. Really, really sorry."

Nikki finally smiled. "Hey, we forgive you," she said. "I guess it wasn't your fault. I mean, it's pretty hard to tell a grown-up like Isabel what to do."

"That's the truth," Amber said.

Haley nodded. "Yeah. I'm still upset about it, but I guess I can't blame you. Like you said, *you* didn't fire Kathy."

"I'm so glad you said that," Amber replied. "I never meant to get all wrapped up with Isabel. I was just so excited to have a sponsor."

"Well, you getting wrapped up with Isabel is a little like us getting all wrapped up in our superstition thing," Martina said. "Boy, did that turn out to be a mistake."

"It did?" Amber asked.

"Totally," Nikki said. "Alex has been teasing me about it so much lately, I had to start leaving my skate lace in my locker. And you know what? We're still landing our star lifts—even better than before. So much for the good-luck lace."

"And I was doing my lucky routine so much that Dan got totally mad. He made me stop," Martina said.

"Hmm," Tori said. "Looks like you guys are out of luck."

"Well, you're the one who said that stuff didn't matter in the first place," Martina reminded her. "And I'm going to prove you were right. Remember that triple toe–double toe combination I couldn't do without doing my lucky routine first?"

Tori nodded.

"Okay. So now I'm going to land it, period," Martina said. "No routine, no four-leaf clover, *nada*." She circled the rink, then lifted into the jump combo.

Amber watched anxiously as Martina completed the first jump. She lifted into the double toe and completed two rotations. She landed smoothly, holding her arms out for balance. "Beautiful," Amber called to Martina.

"Nice job," Haley added.

"Okay. My turn," Nikki said. "Otherwise I'll have to listen to Alex tease me for the next four years." She skated off and immediately launched into a flawless double toe loop–double lutz combination.

Amber looked at Haley and Tori. "Well? Who's next?"

"Not me," Tori said, skating backward, away from the group.

"Okay. I'll go," Amber said. "I think I've been forgetting to do my spin before I jump, anyway. So here goes nothing."

Amber skated off, past Nikki and Martina, who were talking at one end of the rink. She circled the rink until she built up enough speed. Then she dug her toe pick into the ice, lifted her arms, and hit her triple salchow. She landed it perfectly.

"All right!" Nikki cried. "No more Armstrong spin."

Amber skated back to Haley and Tori, stopping just short of them.

Haley reached into her sweatshirt pocket for her purple rabbit's foot. She petted it a few times, smoothing down the artificial fur. "Well, my little friend, it's been fun," Haley began. "But unless I turn you into a necklace, you just won't be coming to the Olympics with me. So . . . *hasta la vista*, baby!"

Haley tossed the rabbit's foot over the boards, then took off down the ice and landed a perfect double axel.

"Well?" Haley said, skating back to Tori. "You're the only one who hasn't jumped yet. What are you waiting for?"

Tori reached down to touch each skate toe, then spun and stretched her arms over her head.

"Hey, no fair! I thought we were all giving up our superstitions," Amber said.

"Yeah—and that looks suspiciously like the Armstrong spin," Haley said.

"So what if it is?" Tori replied. "It helps me land my jumps. Why should I stop doing it?"

"But Tori, remember all those things you said to us?" Amber asked. "About how our luck would run out someday, how it was silly to rely on superstition—"

"I changed my mind," Tori said. "You'd have to be crazy to stop doing your routine now, Amber. Look how far you've come with it." Tori skated away.

Amber watched her go, shaking her head. "I guess I'll never know what Tori's going to do next," she said, grinning. She glanced at her watch. "Well, only a few hours left to practice," she said. "Guess I'd better give this program another try."

"And another and another," Haley teased as she and the others skated off. "Good luck, Amber."

"Thanks," Amber called after her. But she knew it was hopeless. She could never make her new program work in time for her audition on Monday. She was going to fail for sure.

But at least I have my friends back, Amber told herself.

12

"**A**mber! Amber, stop a minute," Isabel called across the lobby of the ice rink. She strode quickly up to Amber.

Amber was done practicing. She was exhausted, and all she wanted to think about was her big sleepover that night at Tiffany's.

"Isabel!" Amber exclaimed in surprise. "What are you doing here? I thought you went home hours ago."

"Not me," Isabel told her. "It took a while, but I managed to arrange more private ice time for us. Tomorrow morning, first thing. Isn't it great?" she asked excitedly. "We'll iron out that program for sure." She gave Amber a pleased smile and waited for her reaction.

"Um . . . tomorrow morning?" Amber asked.

Isabel nodded. "Not quite as early as today. Seven o'clock."

"But I can't be here at seven tomorrow. I'm going to a sleepover tonight, at my friend Tiffany's," Amber said. "I told you about it, remember?"

"A sleepover?" Isabel sounded shocked. "But Amber, that's—that's impossible. You have an audition for a major role coming up."

"But the audition isn't until Monday," Amber pointed out.

"Yes, and tomorrow's lesson is the last chance you'll have to work on your new program before then," Isabel said, ignoring Amber's frustrated expression.

"Okay, okay. I'll make sure I'm here at seven," Amber said.

"Oh, no. That's not good enough," Isabel told her. "You can't go to the sleepover at all. You'll stay up late and you'll be groggy tomorrow. You won't give your lesson one hundred percent."

"But—you didn't think I was out too late when you took me to dinner that time, to celebrate making seniors," Amber argued.

"That was a completely different situation," Isabel said. She folded her arms across her chest. "You'll have to tell your friend you can't make it."

"I—I can't do that," Amber said. "I already told her I'm coming. And I haven't seen her in so long. I *want* to go."

"*She* can adjust her plans," Isabel said icily. "*You*

don't have that luxury. Amber, you're a serious athlete and Monday's audition is an important step toward your future. Do you want to be a winner or not?"

"Of course I do," Amber said. "You know I do."

"Well, then." Isabel rummaged in her purse and pulled out a quarter. "This is for the phone," she said. "If it were up to me, I'd call Tiffany and tell her you can't come. But it's your choice. Just think about that audition, Amber." Isabel handed Amber the coin and turned away, heading for the snack bar.

Amber stared after her, tears brimming. The last thing she wanted was to hurt Tiffany's feelings. But if she went to the sleepover, Isabel wouldn't forgive her.

And Isabel was right—she did need more practice if she wanted to win on Monday. And she needed Isabel to continue being her sponsor.

Amber clutched the quarter. She lifted her skate bag onto her shoulder and went down the hall to call Tiffany and cancel their plans.

Monday morning seemed to come sooner than Amber expected. She paced nervously beside the rink and smoothed the skirt of her new black skating dress. She reached up to adjust the black-and-white ribbon in her hair.

"You really should be wearing more makeup," Isabel said, squinting at Amber's pale face. She sighed and leaned over to tug at the sleeves of Amber's dress. "I suppose we'll take care of that *after* you win the role."

Amber wished she felt as confident as Isabel did. Win the role? she thought. I'll be lucky if I can remember my program.

Her stomach was a bundle of nerves. It was strange. Amber didn't usually get stage fright when she competed. But she had always felt better prepared.

"You look great. How do you feel?" Isabel asked. "Ready to wow the judges?"

Amber shrugged. "Sure, I guess."

"You guess?" Isabel said. "What's that all about? Amber, you and I both know you're better than anyone here today. Including Tori. Don't guess. Just nail your program, and then consider yourself the star of the ice show. Okay?" She gave Amber a quick hug.

Amber felt even more nervous. Isabel clearly expected her to win. But what if she didn't? "Listen, Isabel, I don't feel too sure of my program," Amber said. "I—"

"Oh—excuse me, Amber," Isabel cut her off. "I just spotted an old friend. I'll go say hi and be right back." Isabel flashed her a bright smile, then walked quickly toward the bleachers, where a table had been set up for the audition judges.

Amber was surprised to see Isabel walk up to a

woman who was sitting at the judges' table. Isabel whispered something in the woman's ear. They both laughed loudly.

I'm glad they're having a good time, Amber thought, frowning. Because I'm sure not!

She raised her eyes. Her friends from Silver Blades were sitting in the bleachers. She felt great that they had come to watch the auditions. Amber saw her mother higher up in the bleachers, reading a magazine while she waited for the skating to begin. Amber was glad she was there but also kind of surprised she'd come. Her mom had been so angry with her since their argument Saturday morning. Amber had apologized that night, but things were still a bit awkward between them.

Amber took a deep breath to steady her nerves. Thinking about problems with her mom wouldn't help. Not at all. She crossed the rink to the water fountain around the corner from the girls' locker room. She leaned over to get a drink, then heard voices behind her as someone entered the hallway.

"Mom, I'm tired. And I feel kind of dizzy."

It was Tori.

"You're fine, Tori," Mrs. Carsen insisted. "It's just nerves."

"I'm not fine," Tori said. She groaned. "I think I'm getting the flu."

Amber paused, her mouth full of water. Tori really sounded sick.

"Maybe it is the flu or a cold. But you can get through the next half hour. Then we'll go home and you can rest," Mrs. Carsen promised.

"But Mom—"

"Tori, just hold it together for thirty more minutes. That's all I'm asking. Just audition," Mrs. Carsen said. "Now, come on back inside the locker room. I want to put more blush on your cheeks. You're as pale as a ghost."

Amber straightened up and peeked around the corner. The locker-room door swung shut behind the Carsens. Tori was sick! She wasn't glad that Tori didn't feel well. But she did feel relieved. Maybe she *would* skate better than Tori now.

She rushed back to the rink and found Isabel waiting for her. "I just heard that Tori's feeling kind of sick," Amber said.

"Really? That's a shame." Isabel started to smile. "Though I suppose it might make things easier for us. If you skate cleanly, Amber, I can guarantee you'll win the role," she said, her eyes bright with excitement. "There's no doubt in my mind."

"How can you be so sure?" Amber asked.

Isabel glanced across the rink at her friend behind the judges' table. "Oh, I know these judges," she said vaguely. "And it's looking very good for you to win. And remember—you said you'd do whatever it takes."

"What do you mean by 'whatever it takes'?" Amber

asked. Something about the fierce expression on Isabel's face troubled her.

"I mean that you'll skate your best, of course," Isabel said. "What else would I mean?"

"I don't know," Amber said. "You just sounded kind of mysterious, that's all."

"There's no mystery to winning," Isabel said. "You just have to do your best."

A voice boomed over the loudspeaker. "All right, everyone, I think we're ready to get started." The voice belonged to Dan Trapp, one of the Silver Blades coaches. "We'll go in alphabetical order, which means our first competitor will be Amber Armstrong."

Amber felt her stomach jump. She sucked in her breath.

"You're the best," Isabel said, squeezing Amber's hand. "Good luck."

"Thanks," Amber said. She stepped onto the ice. For a moment, she thought about doing her good-luck spin.

I don't need it, she thought. She took her opening pose and the music began with a loud drumbeat. Amber took a few deep breaths. The music began and she thrust her arms out, pretending she was tossing flowers. She launched herself into the triple flip. She landed it cleanly, then performed a triple lutz–double toe loop combination.

So far, so good, she told herself. The music slowed

and she waved her arms in the air. She still felt silly doing the new moves, but at least her jumps had been good.

Next, I prepare for . . . Her mind went blank. She couldn't remember what she was supposed to do next. She felt a burst of panic. Her body moved forward, her skates pumping over the ice as she moved blindly into a spiral spin. She had to do something.

She was aware that the judges were watching her. Could they tell she was lost? It seemed as though time had frozen, but her brain was racing furiously. What came next? What came next? She was amazed when she realized that she was still coming out of the spiral.

I have to do something else, she thought. But what?

A voice in her head seemed to speak to her: If you can't remember your new program, do your old program. It's better than nothing.

Amber moved into a set of forward crossovers, then began the sequence of moves that came halfway through her old program. They didn't quite go with the music, but they didn't clash with it, either. She made a few small changes as she skated, adjusting to the slower tempo. She performed two more triple jumps.

She heard the clang of the cymbals that meant the music was almost over. She prepared and then threw herself into a triple-triple combination jump. She landed cleanly and raised her head dramatically.

Done, she thought. And for a second, it was all that mattered.

She heard her mother cheering from the bleachers. The other kids from Silver Blades clapped politely. Amber took a bow, then skated quickly off the ice. Isabel was waiting at the boards.

"What happened out there?" Isabel demanded.

"I'm sorry, Isabel. I had to do it," Amber explained. "I completely forgot the program. I couldn't just stop skating."

"But how could you forget? We went over it a hundred times," Isabel said.

"I know," Amber said. "But it just never felt natural, and I got stuck. Really, it's a lot to remember. Especially since I only had one week to learn it."

"I guess," Isabel finally said.

"It was the best I could do," Amber argued. "Really!"

"I didn't like seeing your old program again," Isabel said. "But I suppose you did the best you could. Actually, you looked terrific."

"Really? It was okay?"

Isabel smiled. "It was. I was surprised, of course, but I don't suppose anyone else noticed that anything was wrong."

"Thank goodness for that," Amber murmured.

"Just don't pull that in the Olympics, okay?" Isabel said. She tweaked Amber's nose as if she had made a wonderful joke.

Now it was Tori's turn to skate. Amber saw Tori do

a quick Armstrong spin. Then she glided to center ice. Amber's eyes opened wide. Tori didn't look as if she was sick at all. Maybe it was the makeup.

The music began, and Tori pushed off into her opening moves. "She's jumping higher than ever," Amber said to Isabel in surprise. "I'll never beat her."

"She's doing all right," Isabel said. "Don't give up yet."

Tori leaped into her triple-double combination. Amber gasped. "It was perfect!" Amber turned to Isabel. "I'm sorry, Isabel. I really did mess up. Tori's got to win. Her combinations are perfect. She's skating much better than I did."

"No she isn't," Isabel said. "Trust me—I was watching you. It'll be close. But you have nothing to worry about."

"But Tori is better," Amber insisted. Her stomach was churning. She hated losing.

"Stop saying that," Isabel ordered. "I'm sure your performance made a deep impression on the judges. Especially on my friend," she murmured.

Amber stared at her. What did she mean by that?

"Yay, Tori!" Haley screamed from the bleachers. Amber watched as Tori finished her program with a spectacular combination spin.

Amber bit her lip as the judges made notes on their scorecards. They huddled together, talking in low voices.

I really blew it, Amber told herself. I knew I wouldn't remember my program. I knew it!

She felt sick inside. It was so different from the happy, excited feeling she got when she knew she'd done well.

I'll win next time, she thought. Next time I'll be ready. I'll know my new program, and—

"Ladies and gentlemen," Dan Trapp announced over the loudspeaker. "The judges have made their decision. The skater who will be starring in the Greater Philadelphia Winter Welcome is . . . Amber Armstrong!"

13

Amber gripped the top of the boards to keep from falling over. "The judges chose *me*?" she exclaimed in disbelief.

"Amber! You got it!" Isabel screamed. "I told you you had nothing to worry about." She wrapped her arm around Amber's shoulders and gave her a quick hug.

Amber broke away from Isabel. Her heart was pounding in her ears. I couldn't have won! she thought. I couldn't have!

"I—I've got to go," she said. "My mom will be waiting for me." They had planned to meet outside after the audition—win or lose.

"Call me," Isabel ordered as Amber rushed toward the locker room.

How did I win? Amber asked herself. Tori was better than me. I know she was!

You have nothing to worry about. The words echoed in her mind. *I'll do whatever it takes to make sure you win.*

What did Isabel mean by that?

Amber remembered the fierce look on Isabel's face. She remembered how Isabel had talked to that judge. Isabel had said she knew the judges; she had said it wouldn't take much for Amber to win.

What did that mean?

Amber shook her head to clear it.

Isabel cared so much about winning. What if . . . No, it couldn't be, Amber told herself.

But what if Isabel had fixed it so that Amber would win. What if Isabel had bribed the judges!

Amber stood still. *You have nothing to worry about . . .*

That must be it! Isabel had paid the judges to vote for Amber!

She hadn't really won the role in the show. Isabel had bought it for her, the same way she bought her new dresses, new music—even a new choreographer. Isabel thought her money could buy Amber anything. Even a skating career.

It must be true, Amber told herself. It must be.

She reached for the locker-room door, feeling sick. She just wanted to grab her things and go. She wanted to get out of Isabel's sight before Isabel said one more thing about how important winning was.

The locker-room door burst open, and Tori ran out. Mrs. Carsen was right behind her.

There were tears in Tori's eyes. Amber was stunned. "Tori, I—I'm sorry," she said.

"What are you sorry about?" Tori snapped. She brushed her sleeve across her face, wiping tears away.

"That I—That you—That you don't feel well," Amber stammered. She glanced up at Mrs. Carsen, who was glaring at her.

"I feel fine," Tori said. "I'm just disappointed. Anyway, congratulations. You did a really good job." She and her mother hurried off.

Amber stared after them. This wasn't the way she wanted to win. She didn't deserve anyone's good wishes. She hadn't won fair and square. It was all a joke. She wasn't better than Tori. She just had a sneaky sponsor!

Amber pushed into the locker room. She spotted Haley standing by her locker. She took a deep breath and marched up to her.

"Haley? Can I ask you something?" Amber blurted out.

"Sure. What about?" Haley asked.

"Um . . . I have this problem, and I was wondering if you could help me," Amber said.

"Listen, you beat Tori fair and square. It's not a problem," Haley said.

Amber winced. "I wish it hadn't happened."

Haley looked astonished.

"Well, what I mean is, what would you do if you won something that you shouldn't have won?" Amber asked.

"What are you talking about?" Haley asked. "Are you saying you shouldn't have won the role?"

"Yes." Amber's voice came out weak and whispery.

"But you skated great. You *deserved* to win." Haley leaned closer and lowered her voice. "Listen, don't go around saying you shouldn't have won. It looks like you're fishing for compliments."

"I didn't mean it that way," Amber said.

"I know." Haley picked up her skate bag. "Well, congratulations! I'll see you this afternoon, okay? I'm going to be so late for school!" Haley practically flew out of the locker room.

Amber pulled off her new skating dress and changed quickly into her school clothes. She felt a lump form in her throat. She'd ruined everything— all because she'd listened to Isabel. She'd thought she wanted to win more than anything else, but now she knew better. She was glad she had her friends back. But she also wanted Kathy back. She wanted someone who believed in her for real, whether she won or lost.

She hurried blindly out of the locker room and reached for the glass doors leading to the parking lot. She felt a hand on her sleeve.

"Amber? I've been looking all over for you."

Kathy was standing behind her, a smile spread across her face. "I wanted to congratulate you," Kathy said. "I know you'll do well in that role."

"I—I have to go," Amber said, wrenching her arm away. She pushed through the door, her whole body shaking. She ran over to her mother with tears spilling down her cheeks.

"Amber? What's wrong?" Mrs. Armstrong threw her arms around her. "Honey, what is it?"

"It's—It's Isabel," Amber managed to get out.

"Isabel?" her mother asked. "What's she done now?"

"Everything!" Amber wailed. "I didn't win the audition. Isabel fixed it. She paid for me to win."

"What? How could she do that?" Mrs. Armstrong laughed. "Honey, that's impossible. You're just worn out from all this pressure and excitement."

Amber shook her head. "No, I'm not. I know what I'm talking about, Mom. Isabel paid the judges. You know how much money she has. She really wanted me to win. She really wants my career to take off, but for all the wrong reasons! She—"

"Whoa. Slow down." Mrs. Armstrong squeezed Amber's hands. "You're not making sense. Why would Isabel do something like that?"

"She said she'd make sure I won the role," Amber said. "She said she would do *anything*. And then I saw her talking to a judge—right before the audition. She said it wouldn't be hard for me to win. Don't you see, Mom? She bribed the judges. That's the only reason I beat Tori."

"I don't know," Mrs. Armstrong said slowly. "I'm not convinced. For one thing, you skated perfectly. For another thing, even if Isabel is a little . . . intense about winning, are you sure she'd go that far? That's pretty extreme."

"Mom, Isabel would do anything to make me win!" Amber cried. "Don't you see? She's been doing that all along. She fired Kathy and Blake, didn't she?"

Mrs. Armstrong frowned. "But this is serious, Amber. If anyone found out, your career would be over."

"I know! I'd be kicked out of Silver Blades. No one would ever believe me again, about anything!" Amber started crying even harder.

"Amber! Hold on," Mrs. Armstrong said firmly. "Either Isabel did something illegal or she didn't. But you didn't have anything to do with it."

"Mom, what should I do?" Amber asked. "I want to tell Kathy what Isabel did. I don't want to lie."

"Let me think for a minute," Mrs. Armstrong said. "It's hard to believe Isabel would do something illegal. But if it's true, then Isabel should accept full responsibility—and clear your name. One way or another, we have to find out the truth."

"You're right," Amber said. "But if Isabel did bribe the judges, then she can't be my sponsor anymore. What will happen then?"

"Before we decide anything, we should talk to Isabel," her mother insisted.

"I don't want to talk to her," Amber protested.

"It's the only way, Amber," Mrs. Armstrong said. "We have to give her a chance to explain."

Amber peered at her mother in disbelief. "I never thought I'd hear you telling me to give Isabel a chance. I thought you hated her," she said.

"Of course I don't hate her," Mrs. Armstrong said.

"But look at the way she's treated you, Mom. She tried to keep you away from me completely." Amber dropped her eyes. "And I went along with her. I'm so sorry, Mom. I really am!"

Mrs. Armstrong pulled a tissue out of her shoulder bag and handed it to Amber. "Dry your eyes, honey. You have nothing to be sorry for."

"Yes, I do. I acted like such a brat." Amber sniffled, brushing the tears away. "I've been terrible to you lately."

"Amber, I forgive you," Mrs. Armstrong said. "Look, we'll find a way to work all this out. We're a team, remember?"

Amber smiled up at her. "Right." She was starting to feel a little better.

"We'll go to Isabel's house right after I finish work tonight," her mother said. "Okay?"

"Okay," Amber said.

She had a hard time concentrating at school that day. The hours seemed to crawl by. After school she hurried home and tried to do homework as she waited for her mom to get back from work. But she couldn't think straight. Finally her mother's key turned in the door and her mother walked in.

"I'm here," her mom called. "Are you ready to go to Isabel's?"

"Well, uh, maybe we should call first or something," Amber said.

"There's no point in stalling," her mother said. "You'll be miserable until you know the truth. We'll talk to Isabel first, and then we'll go see Kathy. Now, where does Isabel live? I'll call a cab to take us there."

Mrs. Armstrong checked her address book. "It's 816 Meadow Lane," she said. "That's not too far. We'll be there in no time."

Amber swallowed hard. She couldn't picture herself confronting Isabel. Not after all the things Isabel had done for her. And all the gifts she'd accepted.

But Isabel might have ruined my entire skating career, Amber thought. She pictured herself skating in the ice show. She imagined herself doing the most beautiful, demanding program ever—and the crowd leaping to their feet, cheering and clapping for her. She couldn't let *anyone* ruin her skating career. It was her life!

The taxi came, and they drove into a wooded, hilly section in the wealthier part of town.

"Here it is—Meadow Lane," her mother announced.

Amber spotted Isabel's car parked in the driveway. Isabel was home. There was no getting out of it now.

Mrs. Armstrong paid the driver, and they climbed out of the cab. Amber felt her heart pounding as they walked up the driveway to the front door.

She took a deep breath as her mother reached out to press the doorbell.

14

"**A**mber! What a nice surprise!" Isabel beamed at her. "Ooh, let me give you another hug. You were wonderful—even if you did forget your program."

Isabel wrapped her arms around Amber. Amber stood there with her arms hanging limply at her sides. She wasn't going to hug Isabel back. She shot a glance at her mother. Mrs. Armstrong pressed her lips together.

"May we come in for a moment, Isabel?" Mrs. Armstrong asked.

Isabel stepped back. She kept one hand on Amber's arm. She glanced up at Mrs. Armstrong. "Is something the matter? You hardly look like the mother of a winner."

Mrs. Armstrong smiled but didn't say anything.

Isabel smiled back. "Please, won't you both come in?"

Amber stepped into the spacious house. Her feet sank into a deep carpet. They passed through a small entrance hall and then into a huge living room. Amber gasped in surprise.

The room was filled with skating mementos. There were framed photographs of skaters on the walls and a silver skating statue on the mantel above the fireplace.

Amber peered at the photographs. "Hey, these aren't famous skaters—they're you!" she exclaimed in surprise.

Isabel flushed with pleasure. "Yes, me as a young woman," she replied.

"But—you were in all these newspaper articles?" Amber asked.

"And on magazine covers," Mrs. Armstrong added.

"It's true," Isabel said. "I even won the trophies in that bookcase beside the fireplace."

"Why didn't you tell me you were so good?" Amber blurted out. She stared at the bookcase filled with statues and awards. She gaped at a silver plate with Isabel's name carved on it. "You won the Junior Nationals!" Her mouth dropped open. "You *won*, and you never told me?"

"Is it such a big surprise?" Isabel asked.

"Well, you should have mentioned it," Amber said.

"I mean, I never knew you did so much. All you said was that you once skated!"

"Did you think I just fooled around at the local rink on Sundays?" Isabel asked. "I told you I was a serious skater, once upon a time."

"But Isabel, we had no idea," Mrs. Armstrong said.

"We didn't know how serious you were," Amber agreed. She frowned. "So what happened? I mean, why aren't you more famous?"

"I stopped competing," Isabel said.

"Why?" Amber asked.

"Well, I'm not sure if I should tell you," Isabel answered. "I stopped for personal reasons."

"Like what?" Amber prompted.

Isabel sighed. "Have a seat and I'll tell you all about it."

Amber settled into a large, comfortable chair. Mrs. Armstrong sat on a small love seat. They both looked at Isabel expectantly. "Please, we'd like to hear your story," Amber's mother said.

"All right, then." Isabel paced in front of the fireplace. "I won't tell you I wasn't good enough to go all the way. I don't believe in false modesty. I *was* good enough. But I never made it as far as I could have. My family ran out of money."

"You're kidding!" Amber exclaimed.

Isabel shook her head. "I wish I were. But after I won the Junior Nationals, it turned out that my parents had put all their money into my training. We had nothing left. So instead of going into seniors, I dropped out of skating completely."

Isabel paused. She stroked a framed photograph on the mantel. "That was bad enough. But what was even worse, the girl who placed second to me at the Junior Nationals went on to skate on the Olympic team a few years later."

"Wow!" Amber said. "You must have felt awful."

"I did." Isabel stooped down in front of Amber's chair. "So maybe now you'll understand why I decided to sponsor you. When I read that article about you and Tori, it reminded me of how terrible I felt way back when. I couldn't stand to see the same thing happen to you that happened to me. That's why I came to find you. I didn't want you to have to give up your dreams, just because of money."

Amber felt sad for Isabel. She knew how terrible she would feel if she had to give up her skating dreams.

Mrs. Armstrong cleared her throat. "I understand that what happened to you was terrible," she began. "And it helps me see why you wanted to help Amber. But . . ."

"Go ahead," Isabel said.

"Well, I hardly know how to ask this question," Mrs. Armstrong said.

Amber took a deep breath. "I can do it, Mom." She turned to Isabel. "I know you meant well and everything. But today . . . you totally ruined my life!" she burst out.

"What?" Isabel stared at her in amazement. She glanced at Mrs. Armstrong. "I don't understand."

Amber's mother shook her head. "I think I'll let Amber explain," she said evenly.

"Okay. How exactly did I *ruin* your life today?" Isabel asked. "Because it seems to me that I've gone out of my way to help you."

"Exactly! You've done too much," Amber said. "I didn't want you to bribe the judges to make sure that I'd win."

"I *what*?" Isabel blinked, looking shocked. "What did you just say?"

"You bribed the judges. You paid them off so that I would win!" Amber said.

"I most certainly did *not*," Isabel said in a haughty tone. "Why in the world would you think a thing like that?"

Amber and her mother exchanged doubtful glances.

"Well, because you wanted to make sure I'd win," Amber repeated. "You said you'd *make* sure," she reminded her. "You told me I had nothing to worry about, that you'd do anything."

"Well, I would," Isabel replied. "Anything legal. I'd never consider cheating. Never!"

"You didn't pay that judge who's your friend?" Amber asked.

"Of course not," Isabel told them. "We were just saying hello." She shook her head. "You must believe me, both of you. I would never do anything to harm Amber's skating. Bribing a judge would end her career forever."

"Then I really skated that well?" Amber asked.

"You did," Isabel said.

Amber felt flooded with relief.

"I'm sorry we doubted you," Mrs. Armstrong said.

"I can hardly believe you thought I'd bribe anyone," Isabel told them.

"Well, you have to admit that some of the things you've done have been a little extreme," Mrs. Armstrong replied. "It's not as if Amber came up with this idea out of nowhere."

"Extreme?" Isabel scoffed. "What do you mean by that?"

"Well, you've pushed Amber pretty hard these past few weeks," Mrs. Armstrong said. "And you've made lots of extreme demands."

"Such as what?" Isabel asked.

"You've had her practicing nearly nonstop. You've canceled what little social life she had," Mrs. Armstrong said. "And you've even forbidden me to watch her practice."

"I wanted her to work harder," Isabel said.

"I always work hard," Amber told her. "But the thing I minded most was when you fired Kathy and Blake," she added. "And then you said I should quit Silver Blades. Silver Blades is my whole life."

"But . . . sometimes change is necessary," Isabel said. "I was only doing what I thought was right."

"Change is one thing. When you talk it over with me first," Mrs. Armstrong said. "But barreling ahead with your own ideas, without asking me or Amber how we feel about them . . . well, that's not fine, Isabel. That's *not* what we pictured when you asked to become Amber's sponsor."

"Was I really pushing that much?" Isabel asked, turning to Amber. "I didn't think I was."

"You were," Amber admitted. "I think that's why I blanked out during the program today. It was too much too soon. And I really did want to go to that sleepover on Saturday. It was really important to me."

"Oh," Isabel said. "But I thought we wanted the same thing. For you to win—whatever it takes."

"No. That's what *you* wanted," Amber's mother said. "Amber does want to win, but that can't be the only thing in her life. Her friends are important to her. She has little enough time for them as it is."

"I see," Isabel said.

"And you can't be the only adult in her life, either," Mrs. Armstrong added. "There are others who have important roles. Like Kathy. And me."

"Yeah," Amber said. "I mean, I do have that champion spirit you were talking about, Isabel. I'll practice really, really hard, and I'll skate my best in every competition. But I can't drop out of school, or have all my friends hate me."

"They don't hate you," Isabel said.

"They did," Amber replied. "They were really mad at me because we fired Kathy."

"You didn't fire Kathy," Mrs. Armstrong said. "Isabel did."

"Yes, I did. I thought it was the right thing to do, at the time. I thought Kathy was standing in your way," Isabel said.

"She was being careful," Mrs. Armstrong replied. "Why should we trust you to make suggestions about Amber's skating? You've never been a professional coach. Kathy has—and a good one."

Isabel nodded thoughtfully. "I guess I never stopped to think about that," she admitted.

"Kathy's been a really good coach for me," Amber said. "I miss her."

Isabel looked sad. "I hope you understand, Amber. Whatever I did or said—it was only because I wanted so badly for you to win. Maybe I did push you too hard. Maybe I was trying to make up for the times *I* didn't win."

"It seems that way," Mrs. Armstrong said. "And we understand. We really do. We don't think you're a bad person. But we can't go on like this, with you making all the decisions."

"No. I suppose not," Isabel agreed. "I see now that it's not fair—to you, or your family, or even to me, in the long run. Whatever your decision, I'll accept it."

"Decision?" Amber was confused. "What decision?"

"Whether you still want me to sponsor you," Isabel said. "It's up to you."

"Of course I do—" Amber began.

"But we're going to have another meeting first," Mrs. Armstrong cut in. "With Kathy. And we'll talk about exactly who does what."

"I'd still like to assist Kathy in her coaching," Isabel said.

"I don't think that's a good idea," Amber's mother said. "I think one coach is enough for Amber at this point."

"But you can tell Kathy your ideas," Amber said.

"Well, all right. I'll leave the coaching to Kathy," Isabel agreed. "If you think that's best."

"We do. So, is it a deal?" Mrs. Armstrong held her hand out to Isabel.

"Deal. I'll be Amber's sponsor, for as long as you want." Isabel shook Mrs. Armstrong's hand. Then she turned and shook hands with Amber. "And if I ever start trying to run the show again, just tell me."

"Oh, I will," Amber said.

Mrs. Armstrong laughed. "You can bet on that."

"I still have one question," Amber said.

"What's that?" Isabel asked.

"Who's taking me out to dinner tonight to celebrate?" Amber asked, grinning.

"Well, that's easy," Isabel said. "We both are. That is, if your mother agrees."

"It's fine with me," Mrs. Armstrong said. "And then we'd better call Kathy and set up our meeting."

"Great! Let's go eat right now," Amber said. "I'm starving!" She paused and grinned at Isabel. "Just don't tell me what I should order, okay?"

~ ~

"So it's decided, then?" Kathy asked. It was Tuesday afternoon, and they had finished their meeting in time for Amber's private lesson—with Kathy.

Amber nodded. "Definitely."

"I couldn't do half as good a job as you do," Isabel admitted. "Again, I'm really sorry, Kathy. I got carried away."

"Don't worry about it," Kathy said. "We'll make the changes we talked about, and things will be much better from now on."

"You mean, no more six o'clock practices?" Amber asked.

Kathy shook her head. "Sorry. Those are here to stay." Isabel and Mrs. Armstrong laughed.

"Forget it, Amber," Mrs. Armstrong said. "And you're not getting weekends off, either."

"Hardly," Kathy said. "You wouldn't want that, anyway. But we *will* look for a new piece of music for you—together. And Blake will help."

"No more Philippe?" Amber asked.

Isabel shook her head. "Philippe was a major disappointment. He was faxing corrections for your program every hour on the hour. There's no way he could design a program for you without taking the time to be here. A choreographer needs to work with a skater. I can't believe it took me so long to realize he had no idea what he was doing. He had never even seen you skate!" she explained. "I've already apologized to Blake."

Amber heaved a sigh of relief. Then she realized what they were saying. "Wait a minute. That means I have to start another new program?" She groaned.

"We didn't want to make things *too* easy for you," Kathy teased. "So. We're wasting time here. Let's hit the ice."

Isabel raised her eyebrows. Mrs. Armstrong chuckled. Amber grinned. It was great to have Sarge back again.

"Let's see your layback spin, pronto," Kathy ordered.

Isabel stepped aside, heading for the bleachers. "We'll be right over there. Watching." She and Mrs. Armstrong walked off together.

"Well? What are you waiting for? Start skating!" Kathy said. "Regionals are coming up before you know it."

"Okay, okay," Amber said, pushing off.

Amber knew that she had come a long way in the past couple of weeks. But no matter what anyone said, winning wasn't the only important thing in skating. Winning the *right* way was what mattered— with the right coach and your friends and your family all around.

And maybe your sponsor, too, Amber thought with a smile as Isabel waved to her from the stands.

skater at the school, has a plan that's sure to get her into *big* trouble. Could this be the end of Jill's skating career?

#5: The Perfect Pair

Nikki Simon and Alex Beekman are the perfect pair on the ice. But off the ice there's a big problem. Suddenly Alex is sending Nikki gifts and asking her out on dates. Nikki wants to be Alex's partner in pairs but not his girlfriend. Will she lose Alex when she tells him? Can Nikki's friends in Silver Blades find a way to save her friendship with Alex *and* her skating career?

#6: Skating Camp

Summer's here and Jill can't wait to join her best friends from Silver Blades at skating camp. It's going to be just like old times. But things have changed since Jill left Silver Blades to train at a famous ice academy. Tori and Danielle are spending all their time with another skater, Haley Arthur, and Nikki has a big secret that she won't share with anyone. Has Jill lost her best friends forever?

#7: The Ice Princess

Tori's favorite skating superstar, Elyse Taylor, is in town, and she's staying with Tori! When Elyse promises to teach Tori her famous spin, Tori's sure they'll become the best of friends. But Elyse isn't the sweet champion everyone thinks she is. And she's going to make problems for Tori!

#8: Rumors at the Rink

Haley can't believe it—Kathy Bart, her favorite coach in the whole world, is quitting Silver Blades! Haley's sure it's all her fault. Why didn't she listen when everyone told her to stop playing practical jokes on Kathy? With Kathy gone,

Haley knows she'll never win the next big competition. She has to make Kathy change her mind—no matter what. But will Haley's secret plan work?

#9: Spring Break

Jill is home from the Ice Academy, and everyone is treating her like a star. And she loves it! It's like a dream come true—especially when she meets cute, fifteen-year-old Ryan McKensey. He's so fun and cool—and he happens to be her number-one fan! The only problem is that he doesn't understand what it takes to be a professional athlete. Jill doesn't want to ruin her chances with such a great guy. But will dating Ryan destroy her future as an Olympic skater?

#10: Center Ice

It's gold medal time for Tori—she just knows it! The next big competition is coming up, and Tori has a winning routine. Now all she needs is that fabulous skating dress her mother promised her! But Mrs. Carsen doesn't seem to be interested in Tori's skating anymore—not since she started dating a new man in town. When Mrs. Carsen tells Tori she's not going to the competition, Tori decides enough is enough! She has a plan that will change everything—forever!

#11: A Surprise Twist

Danielle's on top of the world! All her hard work at the rink has paid off. She's good. Very good. And Dani's new English teacher, Ms. Howard, says she has a real flair for writing—she might even be the best writer in her class. Trouble is, there's a big skating competition coming up—*and* a writing contest. Dani's stumped. Her friends and family are counting on her to skate her best. But Ms. Howard is counting on her to write a winning story. How can Dani choose between skating and her new passion?

#12: The Winning Spirit

A group of Special Olympics skaters is on the way to Seneca Hills! The skaters are going to pair up with the Silver Blades members in a mini-competition. Everyone in Silver Blades thinks Nikki Simon is really lucky—her Special Olympics partner is Carrie, a girl with Down syndrome who's one of the best visiting skaters. But Nikki can't seem to warm up to the idea of skating with Carrie. In fact, she seems to be hiding something . . . but what?

#13: The Big Audition

Holiday excitement is in the air! Jill Wong, one of the best skaters in Silver Blades, is certain she will win the leading role of Clara in the *Nutcracker on Ice* spectacular. Until young skater Amber Armstrong comes along. At first Jill can't believe that Amber is serious competition. But she had better believe it—and fast! Because she's about to find herself completely out of the spotlight.

#14: Nutcracker on Ice

Nothing is going Jill Wong's way. She hates her role in the *Nutcracker on Ice* spectacular. And she's hardly on the ice long enough to be noticed! To top it all off, the Ice Academy coaches seem awfully impressed with Jill's main rival, Amber Armstrong. Jill has worked so hard to return to the Academy, and now she might lose her chance. Does Jill have what it takes to save her lifelong dream?

Super Edition #1: Rinkside Romance

Tori, Haley, Nikki, and Amber are at the Junior Nationals, where a figure skater's dreams can really come true! But Amber's trying too hard, and her skating is awful. Tori's in trouble with an important judge. Nikki and Alex are fighting so much they might not make it into the competition. And someone is sending them all mysterious love notes! Are their skating dreams about to turn into nightmares?

#15: A New Move

Haley's got a big problem. Lately her parents have been fighting more than ever. And now her dad is moving out—and going to live in Canada! Haley just doesn't see how she can live without him. Especially since the only thing her mom and sister ever talk about is her sister's riding. They don't care about Haley's skating at all! There's one clever move that could solve all Haley's problems. Does she have the nerve to go through with it?

#16: Ice Magic

Martina Nemo has always dreamed of skating in the Ice Capades. So when she lands a skating role in a television movie, it seems too good to be true! Martina loves to perform in front of the camera. It's a lot of fun—especially when all her friends in Silver Blades visit her on the set to cheer her on. Then Martina discovers something terrible: Someone is out to ruin her chance of a lifetime. . . .

#17: A Leap Ahead

Amber Armstrong is only eleven, but she can already skate as well as—even better than—the older girls in Silver Blades. The only problem is that the other skaters still treat her like a baby. So Amber decides to take the senior-level skating test. She'll be the youngest skater ever to pass, and then the other girls will *have* to stop treating her like a little kid. Amber is sure her plan will work. But is she headed for success or for total disaster?

#18: More Than Friends

Nikki's furious. Her skating partner, Alex, and her good friend, Haley, are dating each other. Nikki knows she shouldn't be jealous, but she is. She'd do anything to break them up. And she knows how to do it, too. But should she? Or will Nikki end up with no friends at all?

Super Edition #2: Wedding Secrets

It's happening! Tori's mom is getting married! Everything has to be perfect—the invitations, the bridesmaids' dresses, and especially Tori's big wedding surprise. No problem! Tori has it all under control. Until she gets a surprise of her own—a new stepsister, Veronica! Suddenly Veronica starts giving orders, and everyone's listening to *her*. Tori is steaming mad. But she knows Veronica is hiding something big. And Tori's going to find out what it is—before Veronica takes over the wedding, and the rest of Tori's life!

#19: Natalia Comes to America

Russian figure skater Natalia Cherkas has dreamed all her life of skating in America—and now her dream has come true! She's moving in with Tori Carsen's family and joining Silver Blades. But as soon as Natalia arrives, her dream turns into a nightmare. The girls in Silver Blades don't want to be her friends. She can't work with her new coach. And she's horribly homesick. Natalia wants to return to Russia—now! So she comes up with a secret plan to run away. There's just one problem. Natalia needs Tori's help—and getting it is not going to be easy!

DO YOU HAVE A YOUNGER BROTHER OR SISTER?

Maybe he or she would like to meet Jill Wong's little sister Randi and her friends in the exciting new series

SILVER BLADES®
FIGURE EIGHTS

Look for these titles at your bookstore or library:

ICE DREAMS
STAR FOR A DAY
THE BEST ICE SHOW EVER!
BOSSY ANNA
DOUBLE BIRTHDAY TROUBLE
SPECIAL DELIVERY MESS
RANDI'S MISSING SKATES
And coming soon:
MY WORST FRIEND, WOODY

LEARN TO SKATE!

SKATE WITH U.S.
A SPECIAL PROGRAM FOR BEGINNERS

WHAT IS **SKATE WITH U.S.?**

Designed by the United States Figure Skating Association (USFSA) and sponsored by the United States Postal Service, Skate With U.S. is a beginning ice-skating program that is fun, challenging, and rewarding. Skaters of all ages are welcome!

HOW DO I JOIN **SKATE WITH U.S.?**

Skate With U.S. is offered at many rinks and clubs across the country. Contact your local rink or club to see if it offers the USFSA Basic Skills program. Or **call 1-800-269-0166** for more information about the Skate With U.S. program in your area.

WHAT DO I GET WHEN I JOIN **SKATE WITH U.S.?**

When you join Skate With U.S. through a club or a rink, you will be registered as an official USFSA Basic Skills Member, and you will receive:

- Official Basic Skills Membership Card
- Basic Skills Record Book with stickers
- Official Basic Skills member patch
- Year patch, denoting membership year
  And much, much more!

PLUS you may be eligible to participate in a "Compete With U.S." competition hosted by sponsoring clubs and rinks!

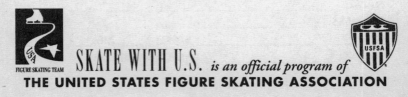

SKATE WITH U.S. *is an official program of*
THE UNITED STATES FIGURE SKATING ASSOCIATION

A FAN CLUB—JUST FOR YOU!

JOIN THE USA FIGURE SKATING INSIDE TICKET FAN CLUB!

As a member of this special skating fan club, you get:

- **Six issues of SKATING MAGAZINE!**
  For the inside edge on what's happening on and off the ice!

- **Your very own copy of MAGIC MEMORIES ON ICE!**
  A 90-minute video produced by ABC Sports featuring the world's greatest skaters!

- **An Official USA FIGURE SKATING TEAM Pin!**
  Available only to Inside Ticket Fan Club members!

- **A limited-edition photo of the U.S. World Figure Skating Team!**
  Available only to Inside Ticket Fan Club members!

- **The Official USA FIGURE SKATING INSIDE TICKET Membership Card!** For special discounts on USA Figure Skating collectibles and memorabilia!

To join the USA FIGURE SKATING INSIDE TICKET Fan Club, fill out the form below and send it with $24.95, plus $3.95 for shipping and handling (U.S. funds only, please!), to:

> Sports Fan Network
> USA Figure Skating Inside Ticket
> P.O. Box 581
> Portland, Oregon 97207-0581

Or call the Sports Fan Network membership hotline at **1-800-363-8796**!

NAME:_____

ADDRESS:_____

CITY:_____ **STATE:**_____ **ZIP:**_____

PHONE: (___)_____ **DATE OF BIRTH:**_____